MURDER, ___NATURALLY

Police Chief Cooper continued. "Anyway, after Stampe burned himself up, he sort of went off the rails completely. Stopped taking drugs and opened up this storefront drug-free place. One of those do-it-yourself encounter things, you know? And he gets pretty good results, too."

I said all that sounded very commendable.

"Oh, sure. Only trouble is, Cobb, this guy commits murders for hire to finance the goddam place! The only reason he's loose is that we've never been able to pin anything on him."

"You said something about his style."

"Yeah. Ever since he stopped pouring chemicals into his body, he's become all-natural. Never uses knives, guns, ropes, poisons, anything like that. He kills on the spur of the moment, using whatever's handy. He did one of his numbers just outside a library in Utica. Beat this guy's head in with a portfolio of bird paintings. The victim had just checked it out. Like I said, whatever's available."

KILLED WITH A PASSION

Also by William L. DeAndrea

Killed in the Ratings
The HOG Murders
*The Lunatic Fringe**
Five O'Clock Lightning
*Killed in the Act**
*Killed on the Ice**
*Cronus**
*Snark**
*Azrael**

*****Published by**
THE MYSTERIOUS PRESS

KILLED WITH A PASSION

WILLIAM L. DeANDREA

THE MYSTERIOUS PRESS

New York • London

All of the characters in this book are fictitious, and any resemblance to actual persons, living or dead, is purely coincidental.

MYSTERIOUS PRESS EDITION

This Mysterious Press Edition is published by arrangement with the author.

Cover design by Dave Gatti

Mysterious Press books are published in association with Warner Books, Inc.
666 Fifth Avenue
New York, N.Y. 10103
A Warner Communications Company

Printed in the United States of America

First Mysterious Press Printing: July, 1987

10 9 8 7 6 5 4 3 2 1

This one is for Jean Brooks-Janowiak, known to her intimates as Elf, during this brief interval in which I am still more famous than she is.

The author extends his thanks to Bill Palmer, holder of a black belt and owner of Bogie's Restaurant in New York, the mystery fan's Mecca, for assistance on some technical points in the preparation of this novel.

CHAPTER 1

"This is a job ... for Superman!"
—Clayton (Bud) Collyer,
"The Adventures of Superman" (MBS)

I had already sent my regrets, but it looked as though I'd be going to the wedding after all. The wedding was set for upstate Sewanka, New York, the last week of April. So apparently, was the Network's next round of trouble.

I sighed and pushed away the pile of reports Marty Adelman had brought me about an hour and a half ago. Marty was in charge of the newly created Network Cable Arts programming system; he was convinced the Network was getting shafted all over upstate New York. As far as I could tell, he was right.

I was in my office on the thirty-sixth floor of Network International Headquarters, more familiarly known as the Tower of Babble. Look at this building from the outside, and you'll see a neat stack of dark gray rock punctuated by tinted windows. Inside, you'll find offices and studios, restaurants and shops.

And a lot of nervous people. Television may be, as some critics claim, an electronic tranquilizer for the masses, but for the people who work in it, it's a stimulant more powerful than any amphetamine. At the Network—at *all* the networks—we deal in three dangerous drugs: money, power, and fame. It's a rare individual who doesn't get hooked on one of them.

I buzzed my secretary. "Yes, Matt?" she said. I run a very informal outfit—first names only, unless we have company.

"Jazz," I said, "ring Marty Adelman and tell him I'm coming down to see him."

Jasmyn Santiago has the proud blood of Cuba in her. She's never gotten over her strict upbringing by refugee parents forced by Castro to find a new home, where they had to live far below their station. She's a walking directory of Network protocol, and she gets very upset with me on those frequent occasions when my dignity slips.

Her position this time was that I should summon Marty Adelman to *me*. After all, I was Vice-President in charge of Special Projects, and he was only Director of Cable Programming, one whole order of magnitude below me. She put it as a suggestion, but it was really a reproach. I ignored it. I heard a frustrated noise before she clicked off, but she smiled and shook her head indulgently as I walked by her on the way out.

Marty Adelman was one of the rare individuals at the Network, one of the unhooked ones. I was the youngest vice-president at the Network—the youngest, in fact, in the whole Corporation. I'm not bragging. I really didn't have much to do with it; it was mostly luck. The jury is still out on what *kind* of luck, but the fact remains that a person my age having my position usually feels a certain amount of resentment from co-workers.

I never got anything like that from Marty. I don't think he even knew his *own* title. To Marty, the Network wasn't really a career; it was merely a means to an end. Marty had been born with the zeal of a missionary; unfortunately, he belonged to a religion that doesn't evangelize.

So Marty's mission became the Arts. He had worked for

Ed Sullivan, spotting top opera singers and ballet troupes for Ed to put on his show. When that had gone off the air, Marty had been hired by the Network as a cultural adviser, in a blatant public relations move.

Marty hadn't cared. He'd worked very hard and had actually managed to get some of his stuff on the air. When cable TV took off and the Network decided it was feasible to program for a fragmented audience (especially for high-income culture vultures), Marty was a natural choice to head the operation.

He was in his element at last. It was a pleasure to see him in the hallways, he was always so happy.

But he wasn't too happy this morning. He had his elbows on his desk and his face in his hands, looking down at something in front of him. "Sit down, Matt," he told me gloomily. "I'll be with you in a second."

I sat and looked around at his framed posters from plays and art shows. Marty was the only person in the building who could have gotten away with that. All the rest of us were forbidden to remove the crap wished on our walls by the Network's official decorator. Instead of a TV, Marty had a big stereo set in his office. He was humming along with the classical music on WNCN.

It took longer than a second. Marty kept reading; every once in a while he'd shake his head slowly and curse under his breath. I think that was one of the reasons for Marty's success: He looked and acted like a regular guy. Many cultured persons I have met I have not liked because they were snobs.

Marty wasn't like that, and his attitude helped him enormously in his dealings with the rest of us philistines here at the Network. He would do everything in his power to get you to like Puccini, but he'd never try to get you to stop listening to ABBA, if that's what you happened to like. He looked like a fairly decent middle-weight fighter a few years into retirement, and he always went around with his tie loose and his sleeves rolled up.

I liked him. That would make the impending job easier to tolerate.

Marty finished reading his report, then slid it across the desk to me. "You don't really have to look at it," he told me. "It's the same as all the others."

"Aced out again, huh?"

"Shafted again, Matt. I'm sure of it. This is the fifth one in a row, over a year and a half now. That report's on Sparta, and that's only the latest. But what the hell am I telling you for? You've read the other reports." Marty tugged at his hair in exasperation, uncoiling heavy brown curls at either side of his head. It made him look remarkably like a buffalo.

"Same setup as the others? Five or six competing applicants for the franchise, all but one or two of whom have agreed to carry Network Cable Arts when they get wired up?"

"Exactly," Marty said. "Only *they* never get the franchise. It's always one of the outfits that *won't* carry NCA who wins. It stinks, Matt. You've got to do something about it."

There was the tiniest touch of desperation in his voice, and I didn't blame him. At last count, the Network had sunk twenty million dollars in NCA, with no profit in sight. It wasn't that twenty million was such a vast sum—in Network terms it isn't; they put that much into a bad situation comedy—it was the fact that if cable systems didn't put NCA on, no one could watch it. If no one could watch it, it would never grow. It would become a Failure. Then would begin the great Network game known among the executives as Covering Your Ass. The first guy to suggest axing NCA would be a hero, and Marty would be out of a job. And the viewers would miss out on all that culture.

It was my job to do something about it. That was the kind

of thing Special Projects was designed to handle. I didn't design it—I just inherited it. Still, I cashed the paychecks; I might as well do the job.

I don't know who came up with the name "Special Projects," but the man was the Shakespeare of ambiguity. I'd worked at the Network almost two years before I was transferred to Special Projects, and I had no idea until I got there what a "Special Project" was.

The basic job broke down into four parts: (a) to keep the Network from getting into trouble or from being inconvenienced; (b) to get the Network *out* of trouble or free it from inconvenience; (c) to minimize the ill effects when the Network *does* get into trouble or is inconvenienced; and (d) to keep anybody from finding out about it.

You may think that this is a difficult job, but in fact it is impossible, especially if your parents raised you with a prejudice against committing actual felonies in the course of a day's work. My people and I do our best.

"Marty," I said, "I hesitate to ask this, but is there any possibility the guys who don't offer NCA are winning these things on merit?"

"No."

"Well. I always appreciate a straight answer."

"Not five times, Matt. Especially when this one outfit takes four of them."

"ComCab."

"Yeah. They consistently come in with higher installation costs and higher monthly fees than at least three of the other applicants. When the towns involved bring in outside consultants—you know, the way they sometimes do—the consultants consistently recommend someone other than ComCab. But ComCab still gets the franchise."

"Okay, I'm convinced. I was before I came down here."

"It stinks, Matt. I hate to bother you with it—"

"It's what Special Projects is here for, Marty," I said.

I hated it, too. Cable TV has the potential to be the biggest advance in communications since television itself. But there is risk inherent in the system. Somewhere along the line, when cable was starting out, someone decided the public would be better served if, instead of letting anyone who felt like it go into the cable business, local governments held a monopoly on cable rights and licensed them to operators. I have always had a hard time understanding why governments always think they serve the public better by protecting them from freedom of choice.

Well, not really. Because the public isn't really what they're worried about. Cable TV is, to put it bluntly, the greatest opportunity for local government corruption since the building of the railroads. The system cries out to be abused. The truly astounding thing is how *honest* most of it has been all over the country. There are some horror stories, but mostly, the cable TV industry/local government story restores my faith in human nature, especially when I manage to ignore the stupidity of the basic setup.

Until now, apparently. It would have to be looked into. Right now, it was the Network that was getting the shaft, even if only incidentally to the main dirty work involved. But an investigation into ComCab would be an investment in good public relations—a scandal in the communications industry makes everybody look bad. It's good to nip that sort of thing in the bud.

Marty looked at me hopefully. "What are you going to do, Matt?"

"I'm going to put my two best people on ComCab, find out who they are and where they're coming from. And what they've done before."

"Are you going to send someone up to Sewanka to monitor those hearings?"

I shook my head; Marty looked disappointed. "I don't want to seem pushy, Matt, but don't you think you should? I mean, you might be able to catch them in the act or something."

"I'm not sending anybody because I'm going myself."

He was honored; he never dreamed I'd just drop everything and see to his case personally.

"It makes the most sense for me to go," I told him. "I know the town. I'm a graduate of Whitten College up there. Besides, things have been quiet in Special Projects lately. They'll never miss me."

I didn't bother to explain that things are usually quiet in Special Projects until they explode into bedlam, with gusts of insanity. The last gust had blown the autumn before, whipping through what was supposed to be the Network's fiftieth anniversary celebration, leaving four fatalities in its wake. Five, if you wanted to count my heart.

But Marty was talking. ". . . hope you can find out what's going wrong and stop it, Matt. I really do."

"So do I. I'll do what I can. This kind of job is like chasing a cloud of steam."

He thanked me and shook my hand. I left him humming again and shaking his shaggy head in time to a waltz. He even showed a trace of a smile.

It was going to be a bitch of a job. Tedious, slow, and possibly unnecessary. It *was* possible (barely) that ComCab had been the beneficiary of a series of coincidences. I would not bet my life against any crazy series of events occurring in this industry. We would also have to walk softly. If we (meaning I) were to get uppity in advance of evidence, or if there was no evidence to find, the Network could be called up on the carpet by government officials on a minimum of three levels. The Network prefers to stay off the carpet.

I was getting a headache already.

But in spite of all that, I didn't dread this thing nearly so much as I dreaded attending the upcoming nuptials of Miss Debra June Whitten and Mr. Grant Sewall, to be held, if the weather prove fine, by the waterfall on the Whitten Estate, Route Seven, Saturday, the twenty-first of April, etc. They'd requested the honor of my presence.

I hit the elevator button and waited, got impatient and hit it again just as the bell went off and made me jump. I said a rude word, got on, and rode back to my office to make arrangements.

CHAPTER 2

*"Like sands through an hourglass,
so are the days of our lives."*
—Opening blurb, "Days of Our Lives" (NBC)

"Matt!" Debra Whitten said. "That's wonderful!"

"I'm not too late then."

"No, of *course* not. We *have* to have you at the wedding. Now that you'll be coming, Rick and Jane will be the only ones from the old gang who won't be there."

I suppressed a sigh. The old gang. An unlikely collection of basketball players and rich kids, thrown together in the artificial environment of a small-town college. I had been one of the basketball players, a New York City street kid with a decent jumper from twenty and a God-given ability to score well on a standardized test. Every year, Whitten College (endowed by an ancestor of Debbie's shortly before the annexation of Texas) finds a kid like that and gives him a scholarship. I was atypical only because I was white.

Rick Sloan had been the catalyst. He was a rich kid and, because he happened to be six-eight and not a spastic, a basketball player as well. Jane Anderson had been Rick's girl friend (now his wife); she had gone to prep school with Debbie. Only one other member of the gang really figured in the situation as I stumbled into it that spring. He happened to be my best friend and one of the two men who wanted to marry Debbie Whitten.

Who was talking to me. "You don't suppose I'll be able to reach them on the phone, do you, Matt?"

I told her I doubted it. I was living in their Central Park West co-op, and even I couldn't get in touch with them.

"They're in the middle of a rain forest in Thailand looking at ruins, Debbie," I said. "I could bring Spot, but he didn't get an invitation, so he might be miffed."

That was supposed to be a joke. Spot is a dog, a Samoyed owned by Rick and Jane Sloan. Part of the reason I'm living in their apartment (aside from the chronic New York City housing shortage) is to keep an eye on Spot while they're out of the country. The Whittens bred Samoyeds; Spot had been born on the Whitten estate. He never showed any signs of being homesick for it.

Debbie thought it was a great idea. "Oh, Matt, *bring* him!"

Debbie's voice had always fascinated me. She was always reaching for high notes to show her enthusiasm, and though the enthusiasm frequently seemed forced (like now, for instance), the notes never did. Despite the flat vowels and nasality of the accent in that part of the country, all the sounds Debbie made seemed to come from her throat smooth and sweet. At times, I thought that was the whole secret of her appeal. Then I would remember that Debbie was pretty, if not beautiful, with blond hair and blue eyes, and a trim, athletic figure featuring truly spectacular legs. I would also remember that her father owned the Sewanka *Daily Sun* and forty-five other daily newspapers in small and medium-sized towns all over the country, as well as the local TV and radio stations in Sewanka. I always wound up conceding there was more to Debbie's attractiveness than her voice, whether she appealed to me or not.

"Do you really want me to bring Spot?" I asked. "It

would make things easier for me. I really can't see an aristo-crat like Spot in a commercial kennel."

"You wouldn't dare put one of our dogs in a commercial kennel!"

"Correct," I said. "I'll have to bring him with me, if you want me to come."

"I really do, Matt. Dan will be so glad you've changed your mind."

I froze. I'd been dreading this phone call because I *knew* Debbie would wind up saying something like this. Dan Morris was the friend I alluded to earlier. He was the last one to join the "gang" Debbie liked to talk about. He'd been my roommate at the dorm; I introduced him to Debbie.

In a life filled with mistakes of greater or lesser severity, that was one of my all-time best. Dan fell in love with Deb-bie Whitten, instantly and hopelessly. He could have had a top career with any computer outfit anywhere, but instead he contented himself with a small consulting business in Se-wanka. He could have been on the Olympic team a few years back—he had black belts in judo (which is an Olym-pic sport) and karate (which is not). The coach nearly cried when Dan turned down the spot on the team, told him he was a good shot for the silver medal, with an outside chance at the gold.

Dan just wouldn't leave Sewanka as long as Debbie was there. He wouldn't give up. And Debbie led him on.

I talked about Debbie's attractions before. Dan, in all the world, I think, saw something in Debbie besides looks, money, and a magical voice. He was embarrassed to talk about it, but then he always was when it came to things he cared about. One time, though, he let something slip. Deb-bie had just canceled out on something Dan had been look-ing forward to for a month, to go off with some guy her mother thought should be shown around.

Dan put down the phone, looked at me, and said, "God,

Matt, that stupid bitch. I bet she doesn't even know how
rotten that is. She deserves—I mean, *I* deserve—better,
goddammit."

I didn't say anything, but I wasn't so sure Dan hadn't
said what he'd meant the first time. He saw all these wonderful qualities in the girl, actual and potential, and it drove
him crazy that, in his eyes at least, Debbie refused to live up
to herself.

That's probably why Debbie kept stringing him along.
It's nice to have someone think you're wonderful (or so I
would suppose), and Debbie was perfectly capable of hanging on to Dan because of the way he always showered her
with approval and affection.

Another part of it was that Debbie's father hated the idea
of his little girl sleeping with, and worse, considering marrying, someone not of Their Set. A. Lawrence Whitten was
an old-fashioned possessive father, and tragedy had only
made him worse. He'd lost his son to leukemia, and that led
him to spoil his daughters even more than he would have
normally. Brenda, the other Whitten daughter, was much
younger than Debbie (I figured she'd be about sixteen now)
and had lost a leg in the same auto accident that killed her
mother. Despite the difference in ages (thirteen years or so),
the competition between the two girls was fierce.

Dan made a handy weapon. When Daddy started worrying too much about his poor crippled Brenda, Debbie could
distract his attention by letting him think he would lose her
to a Jew.

Dan knew all this; he had to know it—I kept telling him,
for one thing. But he hung on. Always there, always available when Debbie got tired of one or another of the rich boys
her family was always fixing her up with. Seven years'
worth and more.

Then, two years ago, something drastic had happened.
Debbie and her latest fix-up, a human Ken doll named Grant

Sewall, had become engaged, much to Dan's chagrin. Then they had had some sort of enormous fight at the tail end of their engagement party. She'd run, as always, to Dan.

I got a phone call in the middle of the night. I'd left the party early because I was going to drive back to New York the next day. It was Dan calling; Debbie was going to marry him instead. I pretended to be happy for him, because I'm not at my best in the middle of the night and I couldn't think of a way to talk him out of it on such short notice.

It turned out I didn't need to. The new engagement was over in two months. Dan came to visit me in New York for the first time since college. He got drunk, and watched Rick and Jane's TV for three days. Then he slept for seventeen hours, got up, and headed back to Sewanka; and while I'd phoned him occasionally, I hadn't seen him since.

That had been over a year and a half ago. Now Debbie, who'd decided to marry Grant as originally advertised, was telling me how happy Dan would be to have me up there.

I fought it, I really did, but the words would not be denied. I swallowed. "Dan?" I said. "What does Dan have to do with this, Debbie?" My voice was very tight.

"Oh, Dan's part of the wedding party. Grant's asked him to be best man. Isn't that wonderful?"

"Oh, Jesus," I said, or something equally diplomatic.

In talking about Debbie, I hope I haven't given the impression she was stupid. She was not. But she liked to *play* stupid.

"Is anything wrong, Matt?" she asked, and her voice was sweetness and innocence, and if I could have reached her neck, I would have strangled her.

"No, Debbie," I said bitterly. "Nothing's wrong. Not a thing." As if she didn't know how just plain rotten it was to exact that last love tribute from Dan, to make him stand up on that altar and smile as the woman he loved and seven years of his life were lost to him forever. After he had once thought he was home free.

Okay, maybe there was some excuse to ditch him. I'd always felt that his relationship with Debbie was doomed anyway, and seven years or not, Dan would be better off forgetting her, if he could. But to rub his nose in it like that . . .

"All right, Matt," Debbie said. Her voice was still musical, but the brass had come in much more strongly behind the woodwinds. Debbie was playing dumb no longer.

"Listen," Debbie went on. "I know you care about Dan. So do I."

"I said, "Mmm."

"I *do,* damn you!" She was angry now. "And if *Dan* can be a good sport about it, I'd like to know why you can't, too!"

A *good sport,* for God's sake. "Dan loves you, Debbie."

"But you don't like me at all, do you, Matt?" She was very sad now. "You never have liked me, have you? I wish you would tell me why."

She probably thought she meant that. "Don't put words in my mouth. How's the old town?"

"Quiet but fine." She seemed as glad to change the subject as I was. I asked her how Brenda was; she said the doctor had decided Brenda was near enough to full grown to be fitted with her absolute ultimate artificial leg. "She told me, now that I think of it, that she wants to dance with you at the reception."

"Tell her it's a deal. If I'm still invited, that is."

"Don't be stupid. Of course you're still invited." Debbie sounded weary. "When can I expect you? I'll have the VIP kennel ready for Spot. Or, if he likes it better, we'll let him stay in the house."

"I'm not sure yet when I can make it. I've got some business up there. Tuesday or Wednesday, I guess."

"All right," she sang. Everything was apparently hunky-dory again. "The sooner, the better."

Right, I thought, as I said good-bye and hung up. The sooner, the better. Dan was going to need a friend.

CHAPTER 3

"Where am I?"
"In the Village."
—Patrick McGoohan, Leo McKern, et al.,
"The Prisoner" (CBS)

I drove along Route 17, through what is called the Southern Tier of New York State, though it's miles north of New York City. Somewhere off to my left, amid the rich greens of late spring, New York bumped into Pennsylvania. On this particular stretch of road, I could see little silvery curls of rivers through the gaps in the green.

To my right, I could see the fluffy whiteness of Spot's back. Spot hadn't had this long a trip in an automobile since he'd been brought from Sewanka to New York in the first place, and he was enjoying every minute of it. He'd gone a full fifty miles with his face out the window before I got too cold and closed the car up. Spot was still getting enjoyment from watching the scenery go by.

Since this was the kind of mission where I had to be grateful for small favors, I took a few seconds to be glad I was heading toward a place where everyone already knew the joke.

It was Rick Sloan's joke. A Samoyed is a breed of medium-to-large Siberian sled dog, with a perpetually grinning face, pointy ears, and a huge cloud of pure white fur. When someone wonders why anyone would name such a dog

"Spot" (and believe me, they always do), I have to explain he's named for the gigantic white spot that covers his entire body. It was cute the first hundred times.

The traffic thinned out west of Elmira; we went on west for an hour or so, then headed north. Sewanka is a pretty town; sometime around the end of World War II, all the builders and architects got together and said, "Push Tudor." There had been lots of building since, of course, and Sewanka had its share of steel and glass, but somehow the modern look never got so dominant that a person got the feeling he was living in a giant phone booth, the way you sometimes do in New York.

The ugliest architecture in town belonged to Whitten College. There was a lot of mid-fifties brick among the ivy-covered limestone. Still, the ivy had made a pretty good start on the brick, and eventually it would all look as academic and cozy and venerable as Harvard.

I dropped my suitcase off at the Sewanka Inn (actually a pretty sizable hotel—they'd donated their conference room for the cable TV hearings), then got back in the car and headed out to the Whitten estate, north of town.

It rains a lot in Sewanka, but when the sun is out, the way it was that Tuesday, the sky is enormous. It would have to be to hold those incredible clouds—huge packs of Samoyeds in the sky. We never look at the sky in New York; it's always a backdrop for something—a building, a ship, a fire. It was nice to get away from that for a while.

I was feeling good. I was, in fact, glad I had come. I felt that way for at least a half hour. I mention that now, because it became so hard to believe in light of later events.

I was even happy to be driving one of the Network dinosaurs. The energy crisis has affected everyone in the world except the Network motor pool. Still, outside city traffic, it was nice to have the land-based equivalent of the QE2 around to smooth out the bumps.

The tires made a satisfying crunch on the gravel drive of the Whitten estate. The place is big. It's got as much lawn as a golf course and a decent amount of wilderness, too, including its own waterfall. I drove for five minutes before I could even see the house.

It was hard for me to believe I used to spend a lot of time in that house. Every time I saw it, I'd start to hear the music from *Gone With the Wind*. It was a huge sprawl of white, with a three-story front (columned, of course) and wings of two stories on either side.

Brenda Whitten and somebody else were playing baseball on the front yard. The late afternoon sun gleamed from the fittings of her new leg, from the aluminum bat she held in her hands, and from the stainless steel crutches that lay crossed on the grass.

The new leg must be very good, I reflected. I'd never seen her so far from those crutches before. Those steel tubes with the foam-rubber-padded curves at the top and the black rubber handles jutting out about a third of the way down had always been a part of her life, like a pair of glasses.

But Brenda was standing without them now, hitting out at the soft underhand lobs her companion was serving up. Doing a good job of it, too. It was her right leg that was missing, and she was a left-handed batter, so she couldn't stride into the pitch, but she shifted her weight forward effectively enough, and she had a good eye. She was getting solid wood—okay, metal—on about three pitches out of five and sending line drives in the direction of the house.

As I got closer, I noticed two things. Brenda had become as much a beauty as her sister. Her shorts and top showed off a young, strong figure that had lost a lot of the baby fat it used to carry, and her pretty face was flushed with determination and pride. It was good to see her.

The other thing I noticed was that it was Dan who was pitching to her. He'd grown a beard since I'd seen him last, short but thick, and it hid all of his face from about an inch below his cheekbones. Nobody was going to see his mouth tremble as long as that beard was in place. He was still in great shape. Dan was the classic mesomorph, slightly below average height but having a body made of wedges of muscle of various sizes. I had seen him tear a license plate in half. I am eight inches taller than Dan and have by no means gone to seed, but I couldn't do that.

I stopped the car and honked at them. It was gratifying to see their faces light up as I got out, although I admit it could have been for Spot.

I waved to them and started walking across the lawn. It felt like a carpet under my feet, only cooler. Brenda scampered over to her crutches, picked them up, and started out to meet me. Dan came along, being careful not to go faster than Brenda could. With a big grin shining in the middle of his beard, he looked a lot more like himself.

"Hello, Matthew," Dan said. He decided a handshake wasn't enough and clasped me around the shoulder with a strong right arm. I reciprocated. Spot danced around and yipped happily. Brenda stood by, looking amused.

"I can stand here longer than you can ignore me," she declared. I laughed as I turned to look at her. I liked what I saw. There was a lot of strength in her, in her body, and more importantly, in her young face.

"Hello, Brenda," I said.

"Hello, Matt." She stood smiling, suddenly at a loss for words. She took the sweatband off and wrung it out. When she let her arm fall, Spot snatched the band out of her hand and ran off with it.

"Spot!" I called. He slowed down and looked back over his shoulder at the old spoilsport. "Come! Now!"

Spot didn't like it, but he came. He also knew he was in trouble by the tone of my voice. He walked slowly, hanging his head all the way.

Brenda said, "Oh, let him keep it. I've got dozens of them."

I shook my head. "Can't let him get away with stuff like that. You people raise dogs here, you should know that." Spot had returned. I took the sweatband from him, tapped him gently on the snout, and told him he was a bad dog.

"That's one thing I remember about you," Brenda said. "Can't be anywhere for five minutes without giving someone a lecture."

I couldn't really deny that, so I just grinned. "I'm tickled to see you, too, Junebug."

The old nickname made her smile. "Well, are you just going to stand there admiring my shapely leg, or are you going to hug my sweaty body? Give me a little kiss? Uncle Matt?"

"Of course." Her idea of a little kiss was bigger than my idea of one. When she let me have my mouth back, I told her I liked her batting eye.

"No big deal," she said, but I could see pride in her eyes. "Maybe I could hire somebody to run the bases for me."

"At least hire somebody to run away when you start breaking the front windows of the house. Or face the other way."

Dan handed her her crutches, and we walked back to the main house. Brenda was taking the week off from school. "I can catch up, I know that. Besides, that place is the pits. All girls. Country Day School. What a lot of shit."

I saw her look at me sideways to see if I'd been shocked. She seemed disappointed I hadn't.

When we got up to the house, Dan volunteered to bring Spot around to the VIP quarters that awaited him in the famous Whitten kennels, while Brenda brought me inside. Then, when we'd reached the top of the small flight of stairs that led to the big white door, Dan called me back down. He asked me some foolish question about Spot's mealtimes, then looked me deep in the eyes and said, "I'm glad you're here, Matthew. I really am."

The pain of all seven years was in his voice, but there was more. Something was Going On. I hate it when things are Going On, but I swallowed hard and said I was glad to be there, too.

It wasn't exactly a lie.

CHAPTER 4

"Welcome to my house.
Come freely. Go safely.
And leave something of
the happiness you bring."
—Louis Jourdan, *Dracula* (PBS)

At Brenda's command, I opened the door and walked in. There was none of this nonsense about waiting while a servant was sent to fetch the family to meet me, which I thought was very democratic in a house I had always hesitated to enter without my library card.

The Whittens and young Mr. Sewall were in the great hall or the parlor or whatever it was. Debbie was busily instructing tradespeople how the room was to be arranged if it rained and the wedding had to be moved indoors. She had floor plans that looked like diagrams for a major amphibious landing. Cousin Joan went here, Uncle Harry was not talking to Uncle Albert, and so on.

"Touching," Brenda grumbled at my side. We stood in the doorway as everybody but Grant Sewall continued to bustle. Grant was sitting in a black velvet easy chair looking at an issue of *Modern Bride* magazine exactly as though he expected to find the secret of eternal life in it.

I began to wonder how long it was going to take for them to notice us.

The bride-to-be looked at her plan, looked at the furniture, looked at her plan again, and said, "This is *impossible!* And the weatherman said forty per cent chance of rain Saturday. I've got to get this right."

Grant spoke without looking up from his magazine. "It won't rain."

Debbie said, "How do you know?"

"It just won't." He was still buried in the magazine. It would have been interesting to see if his face looked as smug as his voice sounded. "I forbid it."

Debbie turned an exasperated look at him. "Grant, *darling,* if you can't be helpful, at least get out of the way. All right?"

"You're worrying too much. Darling. Rain or shine, we'll be married. That's the important part, isn't it?"

Debbie played her musical voice pizzicato. "I wonder sometimes. This should be the most beautiful day of our lives." She paused with her head tilted, as if testing the phrase for corniness. Apparently it failed, because the next thing she said was, "Well, it *should*. And you don't seem to care at all. You just—"

Grant looked up from his magazine. Like I said, a Ken doll. Blond hair, never rumpled. Blue eyes. Square jaw with the tiniest hint of a dimple in it. The only other person I ever saw Grant's age who was that handsome and that well groomed used to sing hymns on "The Lawrence Welk Show."

He looked at his fiancée. "You know how much I care, Debbie." He said it with no inflection whatever. It could have been a touching declaration of love or a nice vicious piece of satirical ambiguity.

Debbie was voting with the latter. "I know, all right, damn you. You walked out on me once, made me a laughingstock in front of the whole world! Why I took you back—"

"I thought we weren't going to talk about that anymore. Darling."

Debbie was winding up for a good one. A. Lawrence Whitten tried to calm things with a tentative, "Now, children," but it was Brenda who headed off the fight.

"*Hello-oo!*" she bellowed. "Look who's here!"

That got us noticed. Every head in the room but the busts of old Whittens on the mantel turned to us with a guilty look on the front of it. Even the tradespeople, who had no doubt long since stopped hearing family spats in houses where a wedding was imminent, looked as though they'd been caught stealing a cherry off the ham.

All of a sudden I felt embarrassed. I also felt a little disappointed that Brenda hadn't let it go on a little longer, because the details of the fight that had ended the first Whitten-Sewall engagement were still a dark secret, even to the people who'd stayed at the party.

The spell lifted, and the faces all broke out in smiles, as if I'd dreamed the whole thing. Debbie embraced me, Grant and the old man shook my hand. There was small talk. Debbie wanted to know how my trip had been. Grant Sewall asked me how I liked living in New York City.

He asked me that every time he saw me. Despite the fact that Grant was a top executive with one of the largest communications companies in the country and made, at a conservative estimate, 2.46 times the money I did, he was jealous of me because I worked for the Network in New York. He didn't even bother to hide it. It's a pretty common attitude for people in the industry who don't have New York or Los Angeles in their resumés. One of my early mentors told me, "Remember, kid, you can't be King Kong unless you go where the Empire State Building is."

It led to a certain amount of hostility between us. He envied me my job, and I thought he was a horse's ass to be jealous of a crummy job like mine.

I smiled at him and told him that living in New York wasn't a matter of liking. "It's genetically determined. There's a chromosome for it. Been in my family for generations. Now I get uncomfortable when I have to start breathing air I can't see."

That got a laugh, but Grant's eyes were cold, as though I'd put him down. With some people, you can't win.

I ignored him and listened to a gruff greeting from A. Lawrence Whitten. "Nice to see you, Cobb," he said. A lifetime of being The Boss had given him the habit of calling everyone by his last name. "I understand you're doing some Network business while you're here."

I admitted it. "I'm giving a pitch for Network Cable to anybody who'll listen. We haven't been doing very well in this part of the state."

"You're going to lose your shirts on it. Should have made it a pay service. You're never going to get enough sponsors to make money on culture."

"You're just the sort of person to hear my pitch, then. I'm surprised Whitten Communications isn't after the franchise here."

The old man grunted. "I could have gotten it, but I decided it wasn't worth the trouble. I have all sorts of lawyers fighting off antitrust now, because I own the newspapers in this town along with my stations. Why give them more to attack me about? I'll get my share of cable operations."

He gave me a shrewd look. "Why did the Network send *you* to pitch the committee, Cobb? Aren't you Special Projects? What's going on?"

The old guy was sharp. I was still trying to come up with something plausible when I was saved by Debbie.

"Where's Spot?" she demanded. Her father muttered something about that being a damned silly name to give a fine animal.

"Dan's brought him around to the kennels," I told her.

"I want to *meet* him," Debbie said. "Let's go. We'll be back in a minute, everybody." She grabbed me by my wrist and hauled me from the room. Almost as an afterthought, she looked back at the tradespeople. "You may go home," she told them. "Leave things the way we have them. It's not going to rain Saturday, anyway."

CHAPTER 5

"Here's my proposition, friend;
tell ya what I'm gonna do..."
—Sid Stone, "Texaco Star Theater" (NBC)

We left the house the back way and headed toward the kennels. Debbie did not let go of my hand. She was being friendly to the point of coquettishness. Keeping in practice, probably.

"You look wonderful, Matt. Heredity or not, New York agrees with you."

"You look pretty terrific yourself," I told her. "The whole family looks well. Grant should be prosecuted for exceeding the handsome limit, but there's nothing new about that."

"Flatterer," she said. She tossed her yellow hair around her as if to shake the compliments from it. Her face brightened. "How about Brenda? Isn't she turning into a beauty?"

"*Has* turned, I think."

Debbie nodded. "It's a good thing I'm going to be an old married lady. I wouldn't want to start bringing dates around anymore with her in the house. I mean, she was always pretty, but with her...condition, she's always had a tendency to be a little fat."

"She didn't look fat the last time I saw her."

"Oh. When was that?"

Oops. Cobb steps in another one. That stupid engagement party would have been a good topic to leave alone. "Ah, a couple of years ago when I, ah, came up for—"

"Oh, then." Debbie waved a hand to show me she didn't mind my mentioning it. "She'd already started trimming down by then. She was just a little plump.

"But now she's *great*," Debbie went on. "I'm so proud of her. She watches her diet and exercises—Dan helps her with that. He is a darling, isn't he, Matt?"

I looked at her. All I trusted myself to say was "Yes." It occurred to me that she was daring me to make something of it. I left it alone.

"Anyway," Debbie went on, "it's done wonders for her. She used to brood about her leg a lot, call herself a freak and a cripple and things like that, but she doesn't anymore."

I had two reactions to that, neither of which I voiced. One, if I were to lose a leg, I might not cry constantly in public, but I don't think many weeks would pass without my having brooded about the situation at least once. Two, a person who has stopped brooding about something does not mention that something twice in the first thirty seconds of a conversation, the way Brenda had that afternoon.

I smiled all the way through the kennels. One Samoyed can be beautiful, but dozens of them all at once are silly: animated white puffballs, punctuated with black dots for noses and eyes and occasional flashes of pink when mouths were opened.

Dan met us and took us to Spot, who'd already made himself at home in his new luxurious surroundings. He did seem happy to see me, but there was no trace of "get me out of here" in his behavior.

Debbie dropped to one knee and scratched Spot's throat with one hand while she examined him with the other. It was a brief business, but while it was going on, I could see a different Debbie—no more poses of any kind, just a competent young woman doing a job she liked to do.

Dan saw it, too. "Well?" he asked. "How good a job is Matt doing as foster master?"

She kept her attention on Spot while she answered. "Excellent," she said. "Really excellent. His coat is magnificent, his teeth are perfect. Beautiful conformation, even if he is the slightest bit undersized for a male his age." Debbie looked up at me. "I remember you told me once, Matt, that you never had a dog when you were a child."

"That's right."

She shook her head. "Well, you must just come by it naturally. And Rick and Jane have done their part as well. This is a magnificent animal." She ruffled Spot's fur. "Magnificent!" she told him. "A magnificent animal!"

Spot is a pushover for flattery; he never gets tired of hearing how beautiful he is. He began to thank Debbie in his customary way, with a big, disgusting slurp job on her face. He'd only dragged his tongue across her cheek once or twice, though, when he pulled his head back, made that snuffling noise dogs make when they have something in their mouths they don't like, gave Debbie a dirty look, and trotted over to his water dish, where he began lapping noisily.

I was laughing. "This is a first," I told Debbie. "He usually *loves* the taste of makeup. The oil in it or something, I suppose. It restricts the women I can bring home to the ones who don't mind having their makeup licked off."

"By Spot, you mean?" Dan asked, and everybody laughed, including Debbie, who had seemed a little more upset than necessary.

"He . . . he wouldn't like *this* makeup," Debbie said. I thought I caught a touch of ruefulness in her voice.

"So you really think I'm doing a good job?" I asked.

"Yes, I do." She had her hand to her face where Spot had

licked it, as if his tongue had burned her. She turned her head away for a second, looked at her fingers, glanced at Dan for a second, then looked at me with her rich-girl smile back in place.

"Yes, I do, Matt," she said, and she was back to the way I'd always known her. Still, it was interesting, after all these years, to get a glimpse of the girl Dan had fallen in love with.

We walked back to the house. Debbie and I did all the talking, which was unusual with Dan around, but then he had a lot on his mind. He certainly *looked* as though he had a lot on his mind. He walked a little ahead of Debbie and me with his head down and his hands in his pockets. He would have been kicking at pebbles if the Whitten groundskeepers had been so slovenly as to allow any pebbles to be present.

Debbie still wanted to talk about Spot. "I'm very happy about the way he looks, Matt. You might run him a little more to tone up his muscles into tip-top shape, but other than that, he's perfect."

Then she had a proposition for me, or rather, for Spot. "Listen, Matt, let's breed him!"

"Now?" It was a stupid remark, but it was the first thing that jumped into my head. My brain frequently surprises me that way; I hear myself saying things I have no awareness of having thought of. Out of every thousand times it happens, the ratio breaks down to 800 stupidities, 198 serendipities, and 2 flashes of brilliance.

Debbie answered the question, stupid or not. "No, tomorrow. Vanilla—she's our prize bitch—is coming into heat, and we haven't been able to find anyone really terrific to breed her with. They're related in just the right way, too, so it will be good for the gene pool. I'll even supervise it myself. What do you think?"

I told her to go ahead; it wasn't as if Spot were the one

who was going to get pregnant, sticking me with a bunch of puppies to worry about.

"You want to come watch?" Debbie asked me.

I was put off for a second, a little anthropomorphism at work. Then I thought, what the hell, it's not as if the dogs mind, and besides, Spot has been known to sneak in where he wasn't wanted and watch *me* doing it. Let him see what it feels like.

"Okay, if I can make it. I'll be tied up in the first session of that hearing tomorrow until late afternoon."

"Can you be here by four o'clock or so?"

I told her I thought so, but you never could tell. It was arranged that if it looked as if I was going to be too late, they could start without me.

Then she invited me to stay for dinner, but I told her I had to bone up for the meeting tomorrow. I have become a very good liar through diligent practice.

"In fact, if it's not too much of an inconvenience, I'd like to borrow Dan. There are some technical computer questions that are going to come up, and I'd like him to vet my answers."

Dan looked at me quizzically, but he saw I wasn't fooling and fell in with the gag.

We agreed to make it tomorrow night, after the dogs got through. Back at the house, Grant seemed to be glad Dan and I weren't going to be hanging around, Brenda mad (she'd spent her time getting prettied up for us, apparently), and the old man indifferent.

I didn't much care. There were all sorts of currents flying around that house, and I wasn't going to wire myself up as a conductor for any more of them until my old pal had had a chance to let me know just what the hell they all meant.

CHAPTER 6

"Here's to good friends. Tonight is kind of special..."
—Arthur Prysock, Löwenbräu commercial

We went to eat at the House of Hans, a German-style delicatessen to the north of Sewanka. The sandwiches there are a foot across and three inches thick, every cubic inch of them delicious. Some of my favorite memories of college days have to do with Hans's.

That night, we got a great honor: Our meal was served by Hans himself. Hans was a man who understood the meaning of destiny. He was born to be a German innkeeper. He was small and stout, fussy and friendly, with a grin that showed bright white teeth and twinkling eyes.

Hans had been a POW during World War II and had won the heart of an American nurse. After the war, he'd followed his beloved to a new home but fulfilled his destiny by becoming a German innkeeper in the United States. Probably the best one.

"Ha!" Hans said, as he put down his tray. "I read the order in the kitchen. Roast beef and Würzburger. Reuben and Würzburger Dark. Two orders of *Kartoffeln*. It rings a bell. I bring the order myself, and I see I am right. How are you, boys? Especially you, Mr. Cobb—" Hans's use of the word "mister" did not imply any great quantity of respect; he used it more the way a teacher will in scolding a wayward student.

"Especially you," he went on. "Daniel at least I have seen once or twice within the last few years or so. What brings you back here at last?" I started to answer, but Hans cut me off. "Eat, eat your sandwich while hot it stays. I don't mind if you talk with your mouth full."

I never needed much persuasion to chomp into one of Hans's Reubens. Magnificent. Hans baked his own bread, cured his own meat, pickled his own sauerkraut, and for all I knew, mixed his own Russian dressing. He imported the cheese. It was no surprise that the stuff Hans served tasted terrific; the only thing that surprised me was that he didn't eat it all himself.

I got lost in the wonders of the sandwich and the nutty, sweet taste of the beer. Hans had to remind me to talk. I put my table manners on hold, and told him about the cable TV hearings and the wedding.

"Wedding? Who is getting married?"

"Debbie Whitten," Dan told him.

Hans's face lit up. "The blond young lady who raises the white dogs? She is your young lady, *nein?*"

"Nein," Dan said. He took a sip of his beer. "Not anymore."

Hans always got more German at emotional moments. "Listen," he said, taking a chair at the table with us. "We are old friends. When I say it is you boys who have made me rich in my old age, by finding me here, off in the hills, and bringing your college friends—I am a *tradition* with the college students now; they *jog* twenty-four miles from campus to come here, and that is all because of you.

"So when I say we are friends, I am not just blowing the hot air at you. I tell you this: I was a soldier. I loved the Fatherland, but I didn't love Hitler. Every German says that today, but for me it was true. I could have crossed a mountain from my home and been in Switzerland and safe from the war, but I was in love with a fräulein who jilted me, and I joined the army to become a hero and win her back.

"I didn't become a hero. A drunken American captured me while I was relieving myself in a stream. That was the best thing that ever happened to me; there (later, I mean) I met my wife. I was a failure and probably a coward, but she loved me anyway. And I have been a happy man ever since. And the girl I had loved had married a swineherd and was a crone before she was thirty."

He stopped talking. There was an embarrassed silence.

"So now," Hans resumed, "you are wondering what the old fool is trying to say, are you not? It is this: If you are a good and honorable man (as I know you to be, Daniel), and you have a true love for a woman, and she is too big a fool to return it, then you are better without her, and she deserves whatever she gets." Hans got to his feet with a great whoosh of air. "Eat up, now. Whatever you like, there will be no check. But don't forget to tip your waitress. There is no reason for her to suffer for my generosity. I must get back to the kitchen."

We tried to talk him out of putting the meal on the house, to no avail. "Come back before you leave town and eat with me again. I will let you pay."

He walked back to the kitchen. Dan and I talked about what a great guy he was and similar harmless nostalgia for the rest of the meal.

I got an order of Hans's apple dumplings for dessert. I'd just put the first sweet-sour spoonful in my mouth when Dan said, "There's no computer stuff you want to know about, is there?"

"Of course not."

"Then what is it?" He stroked his beard.

I looked at him. "You're actually going to make me say

it, aren't you?" He kept stroking. "All right, then here goes. What is the deep significance of all the veiled references and knowing looks out at the Whitten place? Start with yourself and work from there."

"What do you mean, Matt?"

"Why did Debbie shoot you that meaningful glance after Spot licked her face? Just for instance. What the hell happened at the damn engagement party? Debbie and Grant were just about to go into a nice, dirty argument about it this afternoon when Brenda cut them off. You'd think they'd have had that settled, with the wedding four days away, but apparently not. I feel like I've walked into the middle of a movie, and I don't know if it's a comedy or a melodrama or what."

"It's probably what," Dan told me.

"Thank you. You are a big help."

He finished his beer. "Okay. Look, Matt, I don't *know* what happened at the party. Don't you think I wish I did? Whatever it was, it woke Debbie up for the first time in her life."

And drove her into your arms, I didn't say.

"What about that stuff at the kennel?"

"Oh, that."

"Don't give me oh, that. That was not the look an engaged woman gives a man she has spurned."

Dan took a breath. "I still love her, Matt."

I made a face. "Do tell," I said sourly.

"I don't like her very much anymore, but I love her. You know what that's like, dammit. Monica. That girl with the money last fall."

I did indeed know what it was like. I closed my eyes for a second. I was angry, whether at Dan or myself, I didn't know. One of the many things Dan and I had in common was a tendency to fall for women to whom love was an event rather than a process. It bothered me beyond rationality that he should be as stupid about these things as I was, and I told him so.

He laughed at me. "All right. At least now I know where you're coming from. But don't worry, Matt. After this weekend is over, one way or another, I'm going cold turkey on Debbie. Anything I still owe her will be paid in full by the end of this week."

"One way or another?" I asked, but he ignored me.

"Oh, and about that face business. It's nothing really."

"Tell me anyway."

"I promised I wouldn't—"

"Come on, for—" I had a sudden thought. "You haven't been sneaking off with her at odd moments, have you? A last little fling for old times' sake? Instant therapy for when she gets mad at Grant?"

A light came into Dan's eyes, and I remembered how unhealthy it could be to get this man mad. His hand twitched—it really wasn't much more than that—and the thick glass handle snapped off his beer mug. His martial arts training, the endless squeezing of hard wax, the constant punching of sacks of polished rice, had given him incredible strength.

I met his eyes. "Well, Dan?"

Dan and I didn't lie to each other. You can keep an acquaintance going on lies, but a real friendship requires honesty. Dan's options now were to tell me to screw myself or to answer the question.

"Just once, Matt. Months ago. She had a spat with Grant and came to me, and we wound up in bed. In the morning, she asked me for the phone, dialed Grant's number, and made up with him.

"That's when I decided I didn't like her anymore. That stupid, stupid woman. Why does she act like that? I came within an inch of telling her to find some other jerk to be best man."

"Why didn't you?"

"I don't know, Matt. I don't really know. I remember long ago, I used to have a certain amount of self-respect. Maybe this whole thing is like a funeral for my self-respect, you know? The least I can do is stand there in the church and hear the burial service."

"Stop it."

Dan sighed. "Anyway, the face stuff has nothing to do with that."

"What does it have to do with?"

"Oh, all right, why the hell not? Debbie has splotches on her face."

"What?"

"Splotches. Little purple marks. Her skin gets discolored. Like wine marks, only smaller. They come and they go, tied in with her nerves or something like that. It drives her crazy."

I could see where it would. Debbie was supposed to be perfect, especially in her appearance. Someone asking her what was wrong with her face would be too much to bear.

"She hides it well," I said. "All these years, and I never knew."

"I didn't know for a long time either. She gets this special makeup from a dermatologist. It's got medicine in it that treats the condition at the same time the cosmetic covers it up. That's probably why Spot didn't like the taste. She wears it all the time, even—even to bed. I'd been with her a year and a half before I found out. Big tearful true confession scene, you know, Matt?

"And it's a funny thing. Since she's taken up with Grant again and I'm out, she's always careful to put her makeup on or touch it up when I'm around. Even that night."

Interesting, I thought. Debbie's index of intimacy was her naked face, not her naked body. I wondered if Grant knew about the splotches yet and how often Debbie planned to let her husband see them.

Dan went on. "So that 'meaningful glance' you saw was nothing. Debbie was just checking to see if her makeup had survived the licking Spot gave it. I nodded to tell her it had."

"How do you plan to steer clear of Debbie after Saturday?"

"What's the matter? Don't you think I can?"

"I think you can do anything you set your mind to, partner," I said. That much was true. Any doubts I had concerned what he actually had his mind set on. "All I wanted to know was how."

Dan showed me a weary smile. "I don't know, Matt. I'm addicted. I'll move to New York. Hell, I'll move to Pago Pago if I have to. But I'll do it. I would have done it already, but . . ."

It occurred to me that I'd done nothing this whole conversation but ask him questions, so I deliberately held back the straight line. When Dan saw I could wait as long as he did, he went on without it.

"Well . . . I would have walked out before, but I owe Debbie one more thing."

"*What*, for God's sake?" So much for not asking questions.

"I've got to keep her from marrying Grant."

"Dan, no," I said. I wanted to cry. He hadn't learned a thing.

"*Yes*, Matt, goddammit!" He rattled the table with an openhanded slap. "You don't know her, you don't love her! She can be a wonderful woman, if she gets the chance. Okay, I couldn't make her see that, but I came a hell of a lot closer than Grant ever will!"

Dan was shouting at full volume, and people were starting to look at us. I tried to quiet him down, but when he was in that mood, it was like trying to quiet an avalanche.

"Shut up! This is final! If she marries him, it will be the same as suicide for her. I'm going to stop that marriage if I have to *strangle* her!"

He stood up, nearly upsetting the table, spun on his heel, and stomped out of the restaurant. I sat there and finished my dumplings, alone with my reflections. I reflected that that was one choice bit of logic he'd departed with, and I mused about the consequences of Dan's little tirade if someone in the restaurant figured out what wedding we were talking about and got back to the Whittens with it.

I also reflected that Dan wasn't going any farther than the parking lot because I had the car keys in my pocket, so I took my time finishing. Then I called the waitress over, tipped her generously, and gave her some money to pass along to Hans to pay for the broken glass.

CHAPTER 7

"...just step up to the microphone and tell us what's on your mind."
—Steve Allen, "The Tonight Show" (NBC)

Everything at the hearings next morning went about the way I'd figured they would. The hotel management had moved all the tables out of the Grand Ballroom and put rows of gray-beige folding chairs in their place. There was a rostrum at the front of the room; a bunch of guys in charcoal gray suits who called themselves the Mayor's Commission for Cable Television in Sewanka sat at it, looking solemn. There was a table facing it, for witnesses. The witnesses were solemn, too. I've fallen in with some gatherings that took themselves seriously, but they were Pollyannas compared to this crowd. I started to get the feeling I'd walked into the wrong conference, the one that was going to decide if the human race should be wiped out this afternoon.

I wasn't on the agenda that day, and I was just as glad. Dan and I had spent most of the night talking. He'd asked me what I was going to do now that I knew what he had in mind; I'd told him in all the years I'd known him, neither one of us had ever yet been able to stop the other from doing something stupid, and I was damned if I was going to wear myself out by trying now. That effectively short-circuited the fight.

Having said that, though, I made him promise to keep it rational, if he had it in him. "However great Debbie is or might be, Dan, she's not worth destroying yourself over."

He conceded the point, which I took for a victory. We relaxed after that and engaged in harmless nostalgia again, this time with no undertones.

I was pretty well convinced that Dan would do what he had to do, but he wouldn't carry it to the point of strangling. My mind Wednesday morning was free to concentrate on the meeting.

Not that it took a whole lot of concentration. They were at the point of the process where they were listening to outrageous demands from special-interest groups that wanted their own channels on the cable system.

First, the ethnic minorities: Blacks. Hispanics. Italians. Poles. Okay, not so outrageous. There are significant numbers of all these in Sewanka. They wouldn't *each* get a channel, but you could bet a channel in the system would be set aside to air anything these groups cared to produce, free of charge or for a nominal fee. Still, the wrangling went on.

The gays and the lesbians were scheduled next, but there was confusion about who'd go first. The two groups got nasty about it. At last, one of the commissioners, who was obviously less than thrilled by the whole business, suggested they fall back on the old standard, "ladies first." That got a big laugh, but it did nothing to lessen the confusion.

I tuned out and wondered what Marty Adelman wanted. I'd found a message from him at the hotel when I'd gotten in last night, but it had been too late to call him back. I tried to reach him at his office in the Network before coming to the hearing, but he hadn't gotten in yet.

It was probably something to do with ComCab—he'd told me he was going to work some sources of his own.

Maybe he'd learned something of use—preferably that the whole thing was a mistake, that ComCab was honest, and I could take the rest of the week off.

I studied the specimen who was representing the cable outfit in Sewanka. His nameplate said he was Roger Sparn, and that didn't strike me as something a nameplate would make up. He didn't look crooked—he looked too tired to be crooked. He had bags under his eyes, and jowls, and a moustache that had stopped trying to do anything but droop. His hair was thin, and his chin was weak. His suit was rumpled. He looked like he'd wandered in from a production of *Death of a Salesman*. He could have been a salesman, or a civil servant, or a forgotten clerk in a big corporation.

He sat, sad and silent, all through the morning. Then someone suggested a lunch break. I would have applauded if I hadn't been so relaxed. I pulled myself to my feet and left the Grand Ballroom. Just outside, I felt a hand on my shoulder.

"Mr. Cobb?" The voice was smooth and cultured. I turned and was surprised to learn it belonged to Roger Sparn.

The voice pegged him—that and the surprisingly warm smile that went along with it. The man was an ex-radio actor. You find them in all sorts of fields on the periphery of New York show business, men and women who could read from scripts and sound good but who didn't look good enough or ad lib well enough to make the transition to TV or film or stage or disc jockey work when radio drama died, around 1960.

A few make big bucks as voice men for cartoons and commercials; most of them work as ad salesmen or continuity directors, or they hang on doing Off-Off Broadway and dinner theaters.

Most of the ones I've met, no matter how successful, are kind of sad and bewildered by the loss of radio. One guy I ran into said, "I was Romeo. I was Captain Justice. I was the Red River Kid. Now I'm an ugly little bald guy with a voice."

Sparn was a tired-looking, medium-sized tubby guy with a voice.

I turned around and told him his name, then asked what I could do for him.

"Nothing," he said genially. "Nothing at all. It's just that, unfortunately, we seem to be on opposite sides here, and I wanted to say, no hard feelings. I spent some of the happiest days of my life working for the Network."

"You were on radio, weren't you?"

He beamed at me, all but his eyes, and they even lifted the bags a little bit. It made me feel good to brighten the man's day like that. "Why, yes, I was," he said, "although I must say you look too young to remember me in my heyday."

"I remember your voice," I said, sort of telling the truth. I remembered a lot of voices like it.

He told me a few of the shows he'd been on, but I didn't remember any of them. I told him it was too bad his new company and the Network couldn't come to an understanding.

He shook his head and looked sad again. "Network Cable is a bad idea, Mr. Cobb. You can't support highbrow stuff with advertisers; should have gone pay-cable with it, like with the movie networks, Home Box Office, and the like. ComCab can't devote one of its channels to a service that's going to go bankrupt in a few months."

His voice was getting faster and stronger with every word. I was going to do my bit for the Network, and interrupt him and give him the party line, but he was determined to get out his next sentence. He bowled my interruption over and said, "And that's what I told your Marty Adelman two weeks ago."

That was interesting. "Oh, you've talked to Marty recently?"

"Yes, I came to visit him at his office. He was trying to talk us into carrying Network Cable. I thought I owed it to him at least to visit him and tell him why it was hopeless."

"Decent of you," I said. "But tell me, Mr. Sparn, how is it your company is so successful in winning franchises lately?"

I looked for something besides melancholy in his expression as he answered but couldn't find anything.

"Research, Mr. Cobb. That's all. We find out what the community needs, and we provide it."

"It seems so simple." I tried to sound naïve and impressed, with minimal success. Substitute "politicians" for "community," and what he'd just given me could have been a completely accurate description of success by bribery.

He caught my ambiguity and gave me back some of his own. "It works every time, Mr. Cobb. See you this afternoon." He turned and left me.

I watched him go. He even *walked* sadly. He got me thinking. Why the hell had he approached me? I did not buy his nostalgia for the Network. If he was chock-full of that stuff, there'd be no satisfaction in coming to me about it. I'd been in grade school when the last of the radio soaps went off the air— and my mother didn't even listen to them.

I decided to forget it for a while and call Marty at the Network before I got some lunch. Big mistake. I still haven't had that lunch.

A phone at the Network is answered according to formula. Your secretary says your function and that it's your office. If you ever call me at work, you will hear Jazz say, "Special Projects, Mr. Cobb's office, may I help you?" Someone who works in the department answers the phone with the department and his own name. Executive types like me pick up the phone and just say the name, assuming the underlings have already made our position clear.

Nobody picks up the phone and says, "Who's this?"—especially not in tears. I was about to hang up and dial the number again; I was sure I'd gotten it wrong, but the question was repeated, with anger as well as the tears.

"Is this Marty Adelman's office?" I asked.

"Y-yes," the voice replied.

"*Sally?*" Sally was Marty's secretary, Network standard issue—smart, competent, and unflappable.

"*Yes! Who is this?*" she flapped. I pictured the Network as an inferno whence all but Sally had fled. It had to be something drastic to induce hysteria in a Network secretary.

"It's Matt Cobb, Sally. Is Marty in? Is anything wrong?"

She answered both questions at once. "He's in the hospital!" She started to sob. "He may be *dead!*"

Now *I* was starting to get hysterical. "Dead?" I bellowed. "How? Where?"

"I don't *know!* I think a car. Mr. Brophy just told me he was critically injured, and to switch you to him—Mr. Brophy, I mean—if you should happen to call Mr. Ad—Mr. Adel . . ." The rest of it got washed out in sobs.

"Okay, Sally," I told her. "You switch my call the way Mr. Brophy told you, then take the rest of the day off, or go see the nurse, or do whatever you have to do to calm down."

"Will that be all right? He's a very nice man. I—I want to know what happened."

"Tell you what. I'll have Mr. Brophy report to you personally when I'm done with him. Go to the nurse's office and wait."

She thanked me profusely, then switched the call. Brophy must have been sitting on his phone; he picked it up before the first ring was done.

It's little things like that that reveal Harris Brophy's inner emotions, if any. He is brilliant and handsome, and I couldn't run Special Projects without him, but he is the coldest, most detached, most cynical son of a bitch I have ever had to deal with on a regular basis. For some reason he likes me, I don't know why. I do know why he loves his job. Human folly is Harris's favorite spectator sport, and at the Network, people are always in mid-season form.

"Talk to me," I told him.

"Matt?" That was another sign of agitation. He knows my voice.

"Yeah. What the hell happened?"

"You know about Marty?"

"Sally told me he was hurt, but that was about it. How did it happen?"

"Hit-and-run driver. Got him about two blocks from his house—he lives in Brooklyn Heights—on Atlantic Avenue. The police called here looking for you, but I stalled them off."

"Mmm. How did they like that?"

"Not much, but what could they do about it? I only told them the truth. You *are* out of town, and you couldn't be reached. Besides, I wanted to talk to you first."

"Why did the police want me?" It had taken me a while to wonder about that. Usually, when the Network was tied up in something, the cops got to me sooner or later, but this would normally be handled as a matter of Marty's private life, at least at the start.

Normally. I should give up hoping for normally.

"Marty had a piece of paper in his pocket," Harris said, "with your name on it. It said, 'Call Matt Cobb—*Important*.' "

I thought that over for a little while. After fifteen seconds or so, Harris said, "Matt?"

"What?"

"Nothing. I was just afraid you'd passed out on me."

"Ha," I said sardonically. "Important, huh?"

"That's what the cops said. They seem to feel it is, too. Looks to them like attempted murder."

"No kidding. Stolen car, right?"

"Right. They found it a few blocks away, with the keys still in it."

That was standard. Get duplicate keys, steal a car. Run over the lucky man, then ditch it. A juvenile delinquent will then steal the car, if you're lucky, and you will be nothing but a figment of his imagination as far as the cops are concerned. Assuming, of course, they ever catch the delinquent in the first place.

"There was a witness, too," Harris told me. "Guy closing up his store said the car really chased Marty around before it got him. Practically drove up onto the sidewalk to get him. That's a wide street—plenty of room to avoid a pedestrian if you want to, especially at that time of night."

"Right," I said, but I wasn't giving Harris my whole attention. I was thinking what a nice coincidence it was for Mr. Roger Sparn that he had told me about his visit to Marty's office. Now, when the police went through the file of Marty's appointments and came to Mr. Sparn, I would be there to tell them it was all aboveboard. After all, I knew all about the Network-ComCab problem, didn't I?

I told Harris about Roger Sparn and described him. "Find out about this guy."

Harris said, "How soon?" Harris never doubts he can do anything.

"As soon as possible," I told him. "If the New York cops are that desperate to talk to me, it won't be long before they sic the cops up here on me. The sooner I have some idea what's what, the better off I'll be. Call Sally and tell her to go home."

I hung up. I debated skipping the second half of the session and going up to my room so I could be easy to find, but I didn't want to look as if I had anything on my conscience.

By three o'clock that afternoon, I was starting to get offended. Here I was, ready for them, and they weren't coming. I decided they were letting me stew and waiting to see if I would make a break for it.

There was a recess—one of the committee members had to go wash his hands or something—and I took a walk to the lobby to see what was going on. I didn't notice any cops, but I did see a familiar face. It was Les Tilman, a reporter for Mr. Whitten's newspaper.

I called him over. Les was a youthful-looking guy who was born to be a reporter. He carried his typewriter spread and round little potbelly the way a knight would carry a lance and a shield. He always leaned his head forward on his neck, the better to poke his nose into things.

Les squinted at me and brushed with an ink-stained hand at two or three of the sixteen longish hairs that allowed him to believe he wasn't bald.

"Matt Cobb," he said. "Former basketball star. And debating team star. It *is* you. I saw your name on the list of speakers, but I wasn't sure."

"You've got a good memory." *I* hardly remembered I'd been on the debating team. "Covering this for the paper?"

"Doing somebody a favor. Our stringer got sick." He decided to shake hands with me. "So you work for the Network now."

I admitted it. Les asked me if I had any news for him.

"No, just going to say my piece and hang around till your boss's daughter gets married."

"Uh-huh. And I suppose that explains why the chief of the local police has been giving you the old hairy eyeball for the last five minutes?"

I was surprised. I whirled around trying to see who he was. Amateur night. That's right, I told myself, be inconspicuous.

"Don't worry," Les was telling me, "you'll meet him in a

second. He's walking over now. Hello, Chief," Les called over my shoulder.

I turned again, and this time I saw him. I would never have tagged him for a cop. He wore a red plaid jacket, corduroy pants, and hiking boots. He also wore a corduroy face—it was seamed and wrinkled like an old man's. But his hair was dark brown, and he walked lightly and fast. I decided he was about ten years older than I was, despite the face. I asked Les; he told me I was right and that the face was partially explained by the fact that Police Chief Merce Cooper had slept outdoors every night since 1966. He liked it that way, Les said.

Right now, as Les introduced us, though, I didn't know if I was ready to believe any of this. Merce Cooper was just one tough-looking dude who wanted to talk to me.

"What about?" Les asked.

"Get lost, Tilman," the policeman said. "I'd like you to come with me, Mr. Cobb, if you would." His voice made me want to clear my throat.

"Where? To ask me questions about what?"

"You'll find out when I ask them."

I didn't even respond to that directly. Instead, I turned to Les and asked him who the best lawyer in town was.

"Jack Wernick, but *you* can't hire him."

"Why not?"

"He's the new district attorney. He wants to be President someday."

"Tilman, I'm warning you—"

Les was enjoying this a lot more than I was. True, I wanted to show Chief Merce Cooper that I was the kind of troublemaker who wants to carry his Constitutional rights around with him, even when he travels, but I also wanted the name of a good lawyer, just in case.

"Okay," I said, "who's the second best?"

"E. R. Bowen. A broad, but smart as a whip. She had the chief here on the stand one time—"

I learned then how Cooper slept in the wild without being eaten by bears—he glared at them. Les scampered away after two seconds of a glare that could burn the tarnish off a copper pot.

Then he turned it on me, softened a little but still pretty hot. "I would like you to come to police headquarters with me, *Mr.* Cobb. At the request of the New York City Police Department, I am going to ask you about a co-worker of yours, a Mr. Martin Adelman, who was nearly murdered last night. Okay?"

"Why didn't you say so? Let's go."

I preceded him from the building, but I could feel his glare on my back.

CHAPTER 8

*"There's room for only one
tough bird around here—
and that's me!"*
—Frank Perdue, Perdue Chicken commercial

The Sewanka Police Department had its headquarters in the basement of City Hall. There was plenty of room—City Hall was a huge pile of native limestone carved into the rough semblance of a Greek temple. It was big enough for a city five times the size of Sewanka, but it was built during the Depression with WPA money, and nobody was about to complain.

The cellar was all desks and pillars. I followed Cooper's zigzag course across the room to his office.

Cooper was still giving me the silent treatment; he hadn't said a word since we'd left the hotel. No, that's wrong. He ordered me to fasten my seat belt when I got into the all-terrain four-wheel-drive vehicle he drove.

The silence ended once we were inside the partitioned-off corner that was his office. I noted with interest that he closed the door behind him but didn't let the latch catch. A claustrophobic cop. I'd never met one of those before.

When he was satisfied with the door, he turned to me.

"Listen, Cobb. I don't like New York City. I don't even like the idea of it."

"See, I do like it. Lucky for both of us this country is so big."

"I don't like New York City cases messing up my business, and I especially don't like New York City smartass. You start cooperating right now, or I'll haul your ass up before a judge and start wiping out any fond memories you may have of this town."

I looked at him. "Chief—I mean this in all respect: Where the hell did you come from?"

"State Police, two years ago. This job opened up—I always liked the woods around here—I put in for it, and I got it. You gonna answer any questions for me?"

I didn't answer him for a few seconds. I was reflecting on the remarkable number of quaint characters I've run into during the course of what has so far passed for my adulthood. There was one guy. . .

Cooper broke into my thoughts. *"I'm waiting,"* he said ominously.

"Waiting for *what?*" I'd been waiting for *him* to ask me the questions he was so hot for me to answer.

"Waiting," the chief said, "for you to tell how you're in tight with the Whitten family and how they run this town. How I'd better watch my step or I'll be sleeping in the woods, and not from choice."

How do you like that? I thought. He really does sleep in the woods.

I got indignant. "Why the hell should I bring the Whittens into this?" I demanded.

"It's the usual pattern. You mean to tell me you're not going to run off to the old man and tell him to write an editorial about how the chief of police was rude to you?"

"The day I need somebody to . . . Listen, Chief, you may

have noticed that I've been rude to you right back. That's *my* usual pattern."

The lines in the corduroy pinched back into what eventually became a smile. "So you have. Okay, want to start over? I spoke to the New York cops about you. They gave me a Lieutenant Martin, who knows you fairly well. He says you're okay, but you have a weird sense of humor. I don't. Have a sense of humor, I mean. I don't find one damn thing funny about police work."

"I'll suppress myself," I told him. The chief scrutinized me, trying to decide if that was supposed to be funny, then decided to let it pass.

He asked me his questions; I answered them. It was a refreshing experience. Many has been the time I've lied to the police or held something back, but this time I upended the bag and shook it.

Marty had been worried about ComCab. He'd had a meeting with Sparn a few weeks ago. Now Marty was broken up, practically dead. Draw your own conclusions. It was ironic that Marty's death might help grease the skids for the outfit he was so anxious to stop. It wasn't funny, just ironic.

What *was* funny was Chief Cooper's reaction to my story. The more I told him, the more he looked as if he wished I would shut up. All of a sudden, he had (unless the cops downstate came up with the hit-and-run driver very soon) a large-scale investigation of some very prominent local individuals—namely, the Sewanka Committee on Telecommunications.

He said as much. "But I'll do it, dammit. I've got some good men." He gave me that glare again. "But *quietly,* Cobb, you got that? Don't go talking this up. I'm taking your word for it for now because it's too damn dirty to ignore, but you don't have anything that could pass for hard evidence in a cave at midnight."

"Except Marty Adelman's injuries."

"Yeah, except that. That's evidence of something, not necessarily what you been talking about. Keep quiet."

I said I would. He asked for my word of honor on it, and I was so flattered I gave it to him. He even shook my hand before I left him.

CHAPTER 9

"...The worst is yet to come!"
—William Dozier, "Batman" (ABC)

As the afternoon rolled around and I began to try to think of some way to beg off that dinner, I soon realized there was no reason to. I didn't have a single useful thing to do. It was a hell of a situation—an important network employee attacked, and I had very neatly taken myself right out of the action.

It wasn't that I got a big thrill out of poking around murders or attempted murders; it was guilt. This sort of thing was my job, a nasty one, but somebody has to do it, etc., etc. I should have been out doing it. The way things were arranged now, Harris Brophy was working on the New York end (along with the cops there, of course), and Chief Cooper had his men following up the only leads I had been able to think of.

I began to wish something would happen so that I could have something to do besides sit on my ass and watch. I made the wish once; during the days that followed, I took it back approximately nine thousand times.

Still, Wednesday evening, I was feeling restless and dissatisfied. I fit right in with the gathering. The only person who seemed animated at all was Spot, who had proven himself so lovable he'd been promoted to the post of House Pet, even though he liked his kennel fine. It was a rare honor. The Samoyed pranced over to me and grinned; I knelt and scratched behind his ears as he licked my face.

It was a lot better than I got from anybody else. I got a relatively cheerful hello from Brenda, an ill-tempered grunt from the old man, and zombie faces from both Debbie and Dan.

Uh-oh, I thought. There has been a Scene. Dan shot his bolt, and nobody knows what to do about it. After a second, though, I realized that couldn't be it. Dan *might* have been stupid enough to have tried to scuttle the marriage in the presence of A. Lawrence Whitten, but A. Lawrence Whitten was not the type to have let him hang around after making the attempt.

"What's the matter, everybody?" I asked. "Do I offend?" I didn't know if I did, but I was irritated enough to take a good try at it.

"No, Matt, of course not," Debbie said. "Come in."

I took a second to glance at Dan; he gave me a shake of the head. I felt relieved.

"Debbie and Grant had another tiff," Brenda announced.

"Brenda!" her father snapped.

"Well, I'm sorry. We invited Matt and Dan for supper, and Grant gets so offensive, even *you* can't stand him. And Daddy, you have to admit, that's pretty offensive, the way you feel about Grant."

"That's enough," the old man said.

"Well, it's true! I heard the whole thing, and I couldn't even tell you what the fight was about! And I don't think any of you can either."

She used her crutches as a prop to get out of her seat. "So just because Grant decided he had to run off to catch up with things at the office, there's no reason we have to make Matt feel uncomfortable. Excuse me. I'm going to see how many places have been set at the table."

She walked out, holding the crutches like a rifle over her shoulder. She was wearing jeans today, and all that showed of her condition was a slight limp.

"Well, now," the old man said and went on to apologize. Debbie joined him, adding that she wasn't feeling well, and that the argument with Grant had probably been her fault as much as his, and that she knew I'd be kind enough to make allowances for her. Dan sat on the edge of a chair, flexing his powerful hands and looking at me with a miserable little apologetic grin. I wanted to kick him.

Everything was sweetness and light over supper. Debbie suggested we take a walk out by the waterfall, where the wedding was going to take place. The workmen were supposed to have finished putting up the tents and the extra lights, and she wanted to see if they had.

"What about Spot?" I asked. "This is supposed to be his lucky night, isn't it?"

"Oh, of course. I had him in the house today, and it slipped my mind." Debbie waited while a maid brought the main course, lamb in ginger sauce and broiled sweet potatoes. "Actually, Matt, I don't feel up to it. Tomorrow, perhaps."

For the first time, I understood the phrase "a dog's life." Poor Spot, it seemed, was going to have to do the canine equivalent of taking a cold shower because some *human* had a headache.

"Okay," I said, "but don't leave it too long. He becomes an absolute beast."

It was a long walk to the waterfall but a pleasant one. The night was warm, and the moon would have made enough light to walk by even if the path hadn't been lighted.

It brought back memories. Debbie had had her father put in the lights on the path and over the pool so she could have moonlight swimming parties. The bottom was smooth rock, but the pool was deep enough at the waterfall end to dive into. The water was cold, but beautifully clean. It was fun to slide down the falls, too, a drop of fifteen feet or so, swept along by the foamy current of water.

Behind the falls (Whitten Falls, as if I had to tell you) was a hollowed-out place in the limestone, sort of a half-cave. Every once in a while, a guy and girl would disappear from the general horseplay in the pool and sneak behind the falls. It was great, you and your lady groping slippery bodies behind a shimmering, luminescent curtain while the roaring of the water blotted out the rest of the world.

I was smiling at the memory of it, feeling really good for the first time since I'd gotten to town. The back of that waterfall had been one of the most enjoyable venues of my college education. I was thinking especially fondly of one time with Eve Ronkowski, my debate-team partner. Eve was another scholarship student, a high-cheekboned, red-haired girl from Buffalo. Eve had never been crazy about "the gang," but she made an effort to fit in, to please me. That was before the spring of my senior year, when she decided she hated me.

"Wait," Debbie said. The rest of us turned to look at her. "I'm sorry," she said. "I'm not really up to this. I thought the air would make me feel better, but it hasn't. I'm going to go back to the house to lie down. I'm sorry to have dragged you out all this way."

I shrugged. "If you don't feel well, you don't feel well. If you don't mind, though, I'll go take a look at the waterfall anyway. It's a pretty spot, especially at night. Heck, if you tell me what to look for, I'll even check out what the work-men did."

"No need to do that, Cobb," the old man said. "I can still go out there with you. I know what to look for. I'm paying for it."

"Thank you, Daddy. Matt. This—this whole business has been a strain on me." I had no doubt of that. She looked tired. Her face was pale under her medicated makeup, and her musical voice was almost a dirge.

Her father saw it, too. "On second thought," he said, "maybe I'd better take you back. I don't want to find you later, passed out on the path."

"Oh, Daddy, I'll be fine."

Dan spoke for the first time in a half hour. "I'll walk you to the house, Debbie. Let's go."

He shot me a glance before the last syllable was out of his mouth, a look that said, here goes nothing, wish me luck. I thought he might have picked a better time for his Final Attempt, but I also thought the sooner this foolishness was over with, the better for everybody. I sort of shrugged and sort of nodded, and more or less wished him luck.

Debbie said, "Oh, would you, Dan? That's sweet of you. This way, Daddy can still see if the work's been done. It will take a load off my mind to know that."

Dan took her arm. The two of them headed back to the house as Mr. Whitten, Brenda, Spot, and I walked on toward the waterfall.

A little while later, Brenda dropped out, saying she was too tired. She took Spot back with her, partly to keep her company and partly to go for help if anything happened to her on the way back. She had negotiated this path all her life, day and night, but it was a fact of her young life that she could never be too careful.

It was starting to feel like the *Wizard of Oz*, only in reverse. By the time I got to the Emerald City, all my friends would be gone. I watched Brenda to make sure she was okay on her crutches (she caught me at it and stuck her tongue out at me), then ran a few steps to catch up to the old man.

We walked on in silence until we reached the waterfall. The old man didn't seem in the mood for conversation—he walked with his head down and his lips tight—and that suited me fine.

I could hear the falls before I could see them—a noise like bacon frying that grew to be quite a respectable roar. The workmen had done a good job. Everything that was supposed to be there was there. Mr. Whitten said so. Then he took hold of one of the guy wires of one of the tents, put his foot up on a tent peg, and looked up at the moon.

He had to speak loudly for me to hear him over the noise of the water. I had visions of the ceremony Saturday, with bride, groom, and bishop all having to scream to be heard— "*I do!*"

I didn't have any trouble hearing Mr. Whitten, though. He said, "Know why she went back there, Cobb?"

"She said she wasn't feeling well."

"Not Debbie. Brenda. And don't try to tell me she went back because she was tired. She went to spy on her sister and your friend."

"Why should she do that?"

He tore his eyes away from the moon and looked at me. "Cobb, I've been a newspaperman since before you were born. Do you really think just because I'm old I have to be blind and an ass, too?"

"I never thought you were."

"Well, you damned well act that way. All of you. I know how the currents are running here. Your Jewish friend wants to bust up my daughter's marriage. You want to deny that?"

I threw a pebble into the water.

"You and I want him to fail, don't we?" the old man went on.

"It's none of my business," I told him. And the fact that I was lying was none of *his* business. "Besides," I went on, "even if it were the case, what could we do about it?"

"Nothing legal. I just want you to know I can tell which way the wind is blowing. Maybe you just get on my nerves acting like I'm a silly old dummy who can't tell what his own daughters are up to."

"What about Brenda, then?"

"Oh, she wants your friend and Debbie split up permanently, too. She's had a crush on him since she was a baby." He shook his head. "There is something about a good-looking Jew that women can't resist, have you ever noticed that, Cobb? Never could figure it out. And your friend is definitely good-looking. In a dark sort of way, I mean."

I was looking at the moon now, thinking, God help us, this man controls the primary sources of information in the hometowns of some fifteen million Americans.

"The thing is, I figured he'd get over Debbie long before this. That's why I've never said anything. My experience with Jews is that they stick with their own kind."

"His kind," I said, measuring the words. "His kind, Mr. Whitten, are not necessarily Jews. His are the kind of people who stay friends through thick and thin, who never *ever* let a friend down through their own fault. Who help you even when you're doing something stupid and don't turn their backs on you even after you've done it. He happens to be in love with your daughter, Mr. Whitten, and because of that, she's gotten extra helpings of all these things. Sometimes more than she deserves."

He looked at me as if I'd gone crazy. "Well, of course. Debbie has treated him terribly. I didn't mean any offense, Cobb. Hell, I never even knew you were Jewish in the first place."

I was going to straighten him out but decided it would be more trouble than it was worth. "Let's go back to the house," I said.

We were about halfway there when we heard the screams.

They were loud screams, piercing ones to penetrate from inside the house and this far out into the grounds. And they didn't stop.

I left the newspaper magnate in my dust as I sprinted for the house. The dogs added their wails to the night as I passed the kennel. I slipped once and went down, but I turned it into a shoulder roll, regained my feet and kept going. Even as I rushed toward the house, I was dreading what I'd see when I got there.

Just as I got to the back door, the screaming stopped. "Oh, Jesus," I said. I pulled the door open, sprinted through the kitchen into the main hallway.

I was discarding possibilities as I went. Fire was out. Flood was out. Robbery was unlikely—I hadn't heard any gunshots, and Dan and Spot together, with karate and teeth, would have been more than a match for any unarmed intruder.

When I reached the bottom of the main stairs I heard sobbing. I noticed the only trace of damage I'd seen in the house. Two of the posts in the stair railing had been broken out, snapped in the middle like matchsticks.

I was halfway up the stairs before it occurred to me I might have wanted to take along a candlestick or something for a weapon. I decided not to take the time to go back.

I wouldn't have needed it anyway. Nobody up there was going to hurt me; there was only Brenda, Spot, and Debbie. Brenda was leaning against the left-hand wall of the wide hallway. She was the one doing the sobbing. Huge tears rolled from her face and made dark spots on the carpet. Spot was standing over Debbie, licking her face exactly the way he licks mine when he wants to wake me up.

Debbie was lying on the carpet near the other wall in an attitude of sleep, but Spot was wasting his time. Even from this distance I could see Debbie was never going to wake up. She was small and pathetic, lying there. She was stretched out, but there was still enough room to walk around her without touching a wall.

I noted without thinking much about it that Dan had been

right about Debbie's face and the small purple blotches that discolored it. They stood out very distinctly against the whiteness of her dead skin. They were the same color as the great angry purple welt across her throat that showed where someone had hit her with enormous force.

I wondered if the customary music had been coming from that throat when somebody smashed it.

I wondered where my friend was. "Where's Dan?" I asked Brenda. She looked at me dumbly through her tears.

"Dan!" I yelled. *"Dan!"*

No answer. The big house swallowed up the sound.

CHAPTER 10

"Thank you! And welcome to the fastest half hour in television."
—Mike Stokey, "Stump the Stars" (CBS)

I guess you could call what I was doing over the next several minutes thinking. My brain was very obligingly providing me with a List of Things to Do and even giving me hints as to how to go about them. What it refused to do was draw any conclusions. I was doing all these constructive things without the least idea of why I was doing them.

The first thing on the list was Find Out What Time It Is. That was easy. Through some quirk of my brain, I always know what time it is within ten minutes or so, and I wear a watch besides. I estimated it was nine-thirty; the watch said nine twenty-six. I congratulated myself. Then I decided that meant we'd heard Brenda scream about nine-twenty or so. Then I got on with the list.

The next thing to do was Call the Cops. I took a chance and called 911, the instant police-fire-ambulance number in New York. Lots of cities have installed systems like that, and I remembered Sewanka had been talking about it the last time I'd been up this way.

It worked. A small triumph. I was speaking to the police department in seconds. I thought about asking for Chief

Cooper, but I decided against it. Once I gave them the address, they'd call him. There was no way the chief was going to be left out of *this*. The desk sergeant took my name; I told him what, where, and when; he said men would be there right away. I hung up on him before he could tell me not to leave the scene. I wanted to keep my options open.

"Where's the phone book?" Brenda didn't hear the question, or if she did, she was ignoring it. She was sitting on the sofa, her head between her knees, sobbing. Outside, I could hear her father yelling as he approached the house. "Cobb, goddammit, what the hell is going on?" The voice was still distant and quite breathy, but Mr. Whitten was a determined old man. He'd get here before I was ready for him.

"*Brenda!*" I snapped. She looked up at me, anguished and sullen.

"What?" she demanded.

"Cut out the crying or you'll rust your leg."

She goggled at me for a second, astonished that anyone could be so tasteless. Then she started to laugh. It wasn't the healthiest kind of laughter, but this wasn't the healthiest kind of situation. I'd shocked her into listening to me—that was the best I'd hoped for in any case.

Brenda was still laughing. "Matt, you're *sick!*"

"Brenda, your father's going to be here in a few minutes. A few seconds. We've got to be able to handle him. I won't be able to do it alone. You've got to help me keep him downstairs."

"Me? Downstairs? Why?"

I didn't have time to be anything but blunt. I made a mental note to hate myself for it later. "We've got to keep everybody away from Debbie until the police get here."

There were a million things Brenda could have said in response to that, but if I'd made a list of them, the thing she did say wouldn't have been on it. "Spot's still up there," she reminded me.

"Yeah. He might as well stay. He's evidence." That was more or less true. The cops were going to find dog hairs all over the corpse and the murder scene; they might as well find the dog, too.

"Brenda," I said again, "where's the phone book?"

She was going to ask me what the hell I wanted with the phone book but saw my face and decided against it. "It's in the cabinet the phone sits on."

That made sense. I might have been thinking, but I wasn't thinking any too well. I pulled the phone book from the cabinet and turned to the *B*'s. E. R. Bowen. The best lawyer in town, according to Les Tilman. Next, I reminded myself, to the district attorney.

There was a half-column of Bowens, but E. R. Bowen, atty., was easy to find. My luck was holding; there was a night number. I dialed it, made a mistake, pushed the disconnect button, and dialed again, grumbling. You'd have thought people as rich as the Whittens could have afforded Touch-Tone phones.

The night number, as I'd figured it would be, was an answering service. I gave my name again, said it was an emergency, and asked that E. R. Bowen call me back immediately at this number. The operator said she'd do her best; I hung up the phone and began chewing my fingernails.

I wondered what had happened to the old man; he hadn't come in yet, and I'd heard no further yelling. Maybe the effort of running was too much for him, I thought. Maybe he's lying outside dying of a heart attack. Maybe, I thought, you ought to shut up, Cobb.

He came in just as the phone rang. It would happen like that. I didn't know what to deal with first.

Brenda saved me. She got to her feet, without using her crutches, and lunged across the room into her father's arms. The force of her embrace drove the rest of the old man's wind from him, and all he could do was stand there, holding his daughter and trying to catch his breath.

I picked up the phone. "Matt Cobb," I said.

A woman's voice said, "Is this Matt Cobb?"

Under other circumstances, I would have made a remark, but I wasn't in the mood. I just said, yes, I was Matt Cobb.

"Did you go to Whitten College?"

Great, I thought. I'm in the middle of a murder case, and I stumble into a phone solicitation of alumni contributions. "What the hell does that have to do with anything?" I demanded. My temper was straining to break free.

"This is E. R. Bowen," the voice said.

"Oh," I said. So E. R. Bowen was a woman. Fancy that. Les had told me, but I'd forgotten in the heat of my exchange with the police chief.

"I want to retain you," I told her.

She was amused. "*You* want to retain *me?*"

Good-bye temper. "*Will you stop doing that?* This is important!"

"You don't remember me, do you?"

"No, goddammit, but after this phone call, I'm going to. Do you want to be hired or not?"

The voice was all business now. "What's the nature of your problem?"

"Okay, the first thing I have to tell you is I'm not the client. The client is Daniel Morris, here's his address." I gave it to her, then said, "I want you to go there and wait with him until the police show up."

"He's not in custody?"

"He will be."

"What for?"

"Murder. Probably Murder Two."

"You want me to go to the house of a man who's a fugitive from a murder charge?"

"He's not a fugitive from anything. Look. Get your biggest, toughest friends to go with you, all right? Don't worry, I'll tell him you're coming. If he's home. If he's not home, God help me, I'll need you, too, because I'll be leaving the scene of a crime to go look for him. You'll hear from me later."

"This is most irregular," she said. Lawyers say that all the time. They get disbarred if they don't call something irregular at least four times a week.

"I know it is. The question is, will you do it?"

She sighed, a very soft, very nice sigh. "I'll do it. Let me have that address again, will you?"

I gave it to her, then added, "Somebody today told me you were the best criminal lawyer in private practice in western New York. Are you?"

"Yes," she said simply. "I am."

"Good," I said.

She sighed again. "You haven't changed a bit, have you, Matt?"

I said something brilliant, like, "Huh?" but she'd already hung up.

I didn't have time to worry about it. I dialed Dan's number.

The phone rang. And rang. I stuck my head out of the phone alcove to see what Brenda and her father were up to. They were on the couch. The old man's face, which had been red when he came in the door, was now white and numb-looking. Brenda was crying again, but at least she'd kept the old man busy.

Dan answered on the thirteenth ring. He was surly and his voice was rough, the way it tended to get when he'd had too much to drink. Wonderful, I thought.

"Who is it?" Dan growled. "Leave me alone."

"Dan, it's Matt."

Dan began to cry. I had never known him to cry before.

"Oh, Jesus, Matt, I've ruined everything, I don't know how it happened—I—I just couldn't make things go right—"

"Dan—"

"It's over now. I wish I was dead. I never dreamed it would turn out like this, how could I know? I only—"

"Dan!" I said. "For God's sake, *shut up!*"

He subsided, but it was too late. I should have known this was going to happen. I had now given myself a choice of what I was going to do on the witness stand, because it was damn sure I was going to be a witness in this case. I could perjure myself and deny this phone call ever took place, or I could tell the jury what he said and parcel my best friend off to jail for the rest of his life.

The only consolation was I could now ask the question I was afraid to learn the answer to. It might make things worse, but not much.

"Dan," I said, "what happened here tonight?"

"Don't you know?"

"Humor me."

"Matt, I'll pay for the banister."

"*To hell with the banister!* Tell me!"

"I tried to talk Debbie out of this stupid marriage."

"Yeah, go on."

"Then we had a fight. She told me I was petty and jealous and she never wanted to see me again."

"Then?"

"She told me to get out, and I left."

"Did you hit her?"

"Are you crazy?"

"Did you?"

"No. God knows the little bitch deserved it, but I couldn't hit her. I took it out on the banister on the way out. Why?"

"I'll tell you later. No time now. Listen, Dan, a lady named E. R. Bowen is on her way to your place. You do whatever she tells you, all right?"

He wanted to know more, but I made him agree and hung up. So now I knew Dan was innocent. I knew he was innocent because I believed that under the circumstances he couldn't have faked his reactions with me just now. I also knew I was the only person on God's green earth who'd believe that. Dan was in big trouble.

Because right now, just down a short hallway from where I stood, A. Lawrence Whitten, the most powerful man in this part of the state, was yelling at the top of his voice that Dan Morris had killed his daughter, and that he would pay for it. Dan Morris would pay if he, Whitten, had to kill him himself.

And Mr. Whitten was a determined old man.

CHAPTER 11

"... Now do you recognize this voice from your past?"
—Ralph Edwards, "This Is Your Life" (NBC)

An hour or so later, I was back in the basement headquarters of the Sewanka Police Department. The desk sergeant wanted to know if he could help me.

"I wish you could," I said sincerely. At that point, I was wishing *anybody* could help me. "I'm just here to see Miss Bowen when she gets done talking to her client."

"Ms.," he said.

"How's that?"

"We have to call her *Ms*. Bowen. You'd better, too. She's touchy about it. Sends letters to the chief."

I thank him and sat back down. Great. Dan's lawyer was touchy. All I needed. All Dan needed. I looked at my hand, got bored with it, looked at the other one. The fluorescent lighting in the place made it look green, sickly. Dead.

Which brought me right back to the murder. And the ensuing circus.

Les Tilman, of the Sewanka paper, had arrived before the last echo of Chief Cooper's siren had died, and reporters from the rest of the state, and a good part of north-central Pennsylvania, followed in his dust.

The media, as they say, were out in force. Every once in a while, when things inside got too grim to look at, I'd go to a window and take a peek at the fourth estate. Flashbulbs and floodlights lit up the night every time I did. I wondered idly what it would take to get them to storm the house. Would I have to grab a policeman's gun and go up on the roof to shoot myself, or would it be sufficient just to open the window and scream at them to go away and let the family deal with its tragedy in peace? That always makes for good copy, a good show for the TV audience.

I never got a chance to find out. Chief Cooper called me over to him.

"Call off your dog," he told me.

"What?"

"Your dog. He's standing over the body. Won't let the lab boys near it. The girl says he won't listen to anybody but you."

"Oh, right. Sorry. I forgot all about it."

"Work on your memory," he told me. "You're going to fill me in on the background of all this, aren't you?"

Looking at him, I got the feeling that an answer in the negative would displease him. Not that I planned to be difficult about it. Better he get the story from me than from, say, Mr. Whitten, who was at this moment on the phone to the district attorney demanding Justice or a reasonable facsimile thereof. He'd be happy with anything that involved the destruction of Dan Morris.

I climbed the stairs, looking again at the smashed railing on the way. Spot had stopped licking Debbie's face. Now he was standing in front of her, snarling at some cops who were trying to close in on him. One of the cops had his gun out.

"Put that away, you idiot," I told him. "No wonder he wants to bite you."

"Yeah," he said. "Well, get him out of there. We've got to get to work."

"All right, all right. I just wanted you to find things the same way I did, so I told the dog to stay here until further notice. Spot, come."

The Samoyed became his fluffy sweet self again and pranced over to me. I knelt and scratched his throat for him. He pretended not to like it for a few seconds, because I'd left him alone to do such a nasty job. Then he decided I'd been punished enough, and closed his eyes and dropped his ears the way he does when he's happy.

We rejoined the chief. The cook had made coffee and sandwiches, and Cooper was sitting at the kitchen table with a stenographer, catching a snack. Cooper offered me some, but I refused.

"I don't think I'm exactly a welcome guest here, at the moment."

"Good guess," Cooper said around a mouthful of bread and ham. "Mr. Whitten's been telling me to arrest you."

"That's interesting," I said. "Did he suggest a charge?"

"Accessory. Before, after, or during the fact, he didn't seem to care which. That's just silly, of course."

"Of course," I agreed.

"But I can't say I cared much for the way you tipped off the number one suspect before we even got on the case."

"Tough. He's entitled to a lawyer. Even if he's innocent, which you will eventually see he is—"

Cooper made a noise with his mouth.

"—but, in any case, I called the police first. So you've busted him already."

"You're damn right we've busted him already."

"Went along peacably?" I said. "Didn't try to escape?"

"No. Not that it would have done him much good. My men on the scene tell me they didn't know who was more confused: your friend or his lawyer. Seems she'd just got there before they did. He wasn't talking. On his lawyer's advice, naturally."

I nodded. That seemed like the best course for now.

"Okay," Cooper said. "Now we know where we stand. Right now, I've got a fair to excellent circumstantial case against your friend. I've got to warn you, I expect it to get better. I know the guy is your friend, so if you don't want to talk to me, I can understand that."

"Sure," I said. "Then at the trial, the DA summons me as a hostile witness and asks me if it isn't true I refused to cooperate with the police because I was afraid my friend was guilty. No, thank you. Ask your questions, Chief."

He grinned at me. "The New York cops were right. You are a smart one, aren't you?"

"I've been around the block. Ask away. Or have your minion here put it in writing you decided not to ask me questions. And both of you sign it and give me a copy. I want it on the record that I'm cooperating with the police."

Cooper scratched his head. I had him outflanked, and he knew it. I was willing to talk because there was nothing I could tell him he couldn't find out elsewhere.

I gave him the background first, the whole on-again/off-again relationship between Debbie and Dan. I explained to him how Dan had wanted to talk to Debbie one last time before the wedding, to make absolutely sure she wanted to go through with marrying Grant.

Cooper started to smile. He was putting a big check mark on his mental list, right next to Motive.

Then he asked me about the events of the past few hours, checking me for accuracy against the record of an interview he'd already had with Brenda Whitten.

Apparently, they tallied pretty well. The chief had only one question for me when I finished.

"You didn't hear them fighting, then?"

"Hear who fighting?"

"Morris and the victim."

The victim. Courtroom tricks already. At least he didn't say "*his* victim."

"No, I didn't. He wasn't even around when I got to the house. Why?"

I fully expected him to tell me it was none of my business, but he didn't. He probably wanted to demoralize me. "Brenda Whitten heard voices she says she recognizes as belonging to Morris and her sister raised in anger as she approached the house. She just saw Morris's car driving off as she got there."

"What were they fighting about?"

"She says she couldn't make out words."

"But she could make out voices. Kind of hard to believe."

"Knock it off, Cobb. We're not in court. Besides, you yourself admit he was going back to the house."

"Yeah, you really had to wring it out of me, didn't you?"

"What are you talking about? I didn't grill you, I just talked to you."

"And *I* didn't *admit* he went back to the house, I *said* it!" Cooper's rugged face looked bewildered. He honestly couldn't see the difference. I ignored it and went on. "But who says he didn't change his mind, didn't just get into his car and drive home? Then it might have been someone *else* Brenda heard fighting with her sister."

I was really excited with that theory. The more I thought about it, the more I liked it, primarily because it was the first thing other than blind faith that shed some doubt on Dan's guilt. I couldn't wait to tell E. R. Bowen about it. As soon as Cooper let me go (". . . but, Cobb, don't leave town. You know that, of course."), I called her answering service, and they told me where she was, at police headquarters. I stopped in an all-night drugstore and bought a couple of magazines, then went to City Hall to wait for her.

I waited a good long time. I finished my magazines; then,

finding reality impossible to tolerate any longer, I went to sleep and had a nightmare.

It didn't last long, but it was quite vivid. It took place back at the Whitten mansion and telescoped events into a few breathless seconds. I run back to the house, and Brenda is screaming, and Debbie is lying there dead, and Spot is licking her face. Then the cops show up, and Spot starts to snarl, and I call him, and he runs to me. Then *he rears back on his hind legs and grabs me by the lapel*. (Now I *know* this is a nightmare—where did Spot get thumbs?) The dog starts to yell at me. "Pay attention!" he says. "Pay attention!" Then he starts to shake me. Violently, until my head starts to hurt.

My head still hurt when I woke up. I opened my eyes wide and rubbed my face. I shook my head. It was the kind of dream that could make you want to give up sleep. "Pay attention."

Now, my degree is in English Language and Literature, but I've read a book or two by Dr. Jung; and by God, a dream like that has *got* to mean something. I started to try to figure out what that something could possibly be, but I was interrupted by the desk sergeant's voice.

"Oh, Ms. Bowen," he said. "There's a gentleman's been waiting for you."

"Where, Max?"

I pulled myself to my feet as she turned to look at me. "I'm the one, Ms. Bowen. Matt Cobb. I—oh, my God." I didn't say that last part of it because she was beautiful, though she was—dark red hair, dark blue eyes, a great figure that did wonders for a no-nonsense three-piece suit, high cheekbones, and freckles. I love freckles to the point of fetish. I'm also in awe of people who can look that fresh and alert at four-thirty in the morning.

But I wouldn't have said "oh, my God" because of any of that stuff. I would have thought it, but under ordinary circumstances, I manage to be sophisticated enough to stifle that sort of response.

These weren't ordinary circumstances. I knew her.

"Hello, Matt."

"Hello," I said. "Looks like all that debating paid off."

She smiled. "With you or without you. I still haven't forgiven you for that, you know, Matt." Some of the friendliness went out of her smile. A lot of it. Some of the old anger still simmered in her, apparently. I suggested we talk about it over breakfast; she accepted.

She even took my arm, bringing back memories of moments behind the waterfall. Because E. R. Bowen was Eve Ronkowski, my old partner on the debating team. My partner behind the waterfall. The girl who, the last time I saw her, had vowed that she would hate me forever.

Breakfast looked like it might be an interesting meal.

CHAPTER 12

"I'm a ba-a-ad boy!"
—Lou Costello, "The Abbott and Costello Show"
   (Syndicated)

Eve had a grapefruit and black coffee. I had French toast, ham, home fried potatoes, orange juice, and hot chocolate. A look of distaste passed across her lovely features.

I pointed a fork at her. "Resolved," I said. "A man who has been up all night; further, a man who usually skips breakfast altogether, may eat whatever he damn pleases without dirty looks from his companion. You take the negative."

I got a glimpse of a rueful little smile before she covered it with her coffee cup. "You've got a lot of nerve making debating jokes to me, Matt Cobb."

"I never said I didn't have a lot of nerve."

"Besides, the sides of the question are chosen by lot. You haven't forgotten that, have you?"

"No. Listen, Eve. It's been a long time now. If you're willing to forgive me for missing the East Coast Forensic Society Championships, I'm willing to forgive you for holding it against me."

"You forgive *me?*" She was aghast.

"You never *listened*. I told you the minute they paired us

up that if it ever came to a conflict between debating and basketball, debating wouldn't even come in second."

"I couldn't believe you meant it. I thought you were teasing me."

"Why the hell should I tease you about something that was so important to you?"

"That's just it. It *was* important. Do you know that one member of the team who won clerked for a Supreme Court justice? Do you know how much good that sort of thing can do for your career?"

"If you want to be a lawyer."

"Naturally, if you want to be a lawyer!" She thrust her spoon into her grapefruit, sending a fine spray of juice across her sleeve. "*Damn!*" she said.

I pulled a couple of napkins out of the dispenser and handed them to her.

"Okay," I said. "But my learned friend forgets that *I didn't want to be a lawyer*. I was only on the debating team because I used to argue with Professor Payne in class, and he told Dr. Stokes about me. I was more or less drafted. They always knew basketball came first. Hell, I was only there on a basketball scholarship in the first place."

"But you were so *good*."

"Thank you. Street training is what did it. Think fast. Talk fast. Say what the big dude wants to hear, and sound like you mean it. Or lose teeth. I lived with that sort of business all through childhood, so putting on a suit and discussing the merits of this or that piece of legislation was a game for me. It was fun, an adolescent ego trip. To tie people up in knots with their own tongues. But it wasn't important. It never *meant* anything."

"And *basketball* was important?"

"Yes. A sport, not a game. Twelve guys, on the court five at a time. Everybody has a job. You have to believe in each other, help each other. No reservations. No second thoughts. I loved it. If I could have played basketball for a living, I would have been a very happy man. Turned out I wasn't good enough, but I gave it my best. And I always felt good about it."

"You felt good about debating, too." She raised an eyebrow. "Or have you forgotten the crazy night in Albany after we beat those two boys from Williams?"

"That," I said smiling, "had nothing to do with debating."

"You were still happy we won." I remembered the blue sparks I now saw in her eyes. They used to flash in anticipation when one of our opponents would leave her an opening, and in anger when they'd make a point or two on us.

"Yes. But I had just stood up in public and lied for an hour and a half about what I thought this country owed the Vietnam veteran. I agreed with everything the other side said, and I shot it down in flames as soon as they said it. I got tired of that kind of thing, Eve. There's no compromise in a formal debate, no creativity. Nobody tries to find an answer to any of these problems. You just cover up your weak points and rip at your opponents'."

I drank orange juice. "I was *too* good at it. Sophistry considered as one of the fine arts. The science of hyprocisy. It gets to be too easy."

Eve narrowed her eyes and looked at me. "I see. And the conclusion is that that's what I've become. Correct, Mr. Cobb? I failed to make *you* into a professional sophist or hypocrite, but that's what I am, right?"

"It's inherent in the job," I told her. "Somebody's got to do it. I'm not judging you—"

"Oh, no?"

"—but it's the way the system works. My point is, it's not for me and it never was. I've got my own vices. Who's Bowen?"

"My husband."

"Oh."

"Ex. It didn't work out. He got a great offer from a firm in Phoenix, and I had my practice here. I wasn't about to give it up. So he went." She ate the cherry off her grapefruit.

"At least," she said, "I wasn't hypocritical about it."

"Okay, okay, I'm sorry. Poor choice of words. It's just that it kept getting harder and harder to fight for something I didn't believe in. *Anything* I didn't believe in."

I caught her hand. She looked at me strangely but didn't pull it away. I let go as soon as I had her attention. "Eve, look. Just for example, do you believe Dan Morris is innocent?"

"I'm his attorney."

"I know, I hired you, remember? Come on. You knew Dan in college. Slightly, anyway. What do you think?"

"It's not my job to form opinions about his guilt or innocence. I have to represent him to the best of my—"

"All right, never mind. You think he's guilty, but you're going to bust your tail for him anyway. I couldn't do that. Luckily for me, it doesn't come up. Dan is innocent. Between us, we're going to get him off."

She shook her head. "No, Matt. I'm going to have him plead guilty."

I froze. "What did you say?"

"I'm going to have him plead guilty. I think the district attorney will go for first-degree manslaughter. Dan could be out in four years."

"Right. A mere four years. Have you talked Dan into this yet?"

"No," she said. "I want you to do it."

"Are you out of your mind?"

"Damn you, Matt, the police have an unshakable case. Dan was there. He's a karate expert, and Debra Whitten's throat was smashed by a blow of incredible force. Who else on the scene was strong enough to do that?"

"Me."

"You," she said, "are alibied by the girl's father. Besides, the medical examiner says it has all the earmarks of a karate blow."

"Dan isn't the only karate expert in the world, for God's sake."

Eve shook her head. "Matt, you're not thinking. He may not be the only one in the world, but he was the only one in the *house*."

"How did you find out all this stuff so soon?"

She shrugged. It made her hair jump nicely. The cheap lights in the diner brought out nice red highlights. We might have been talking about what movie we wanted to see that night or how to get a stain out of a cotton shirt.

"I'm not positive, Matt, but I think the idea was to get me discouraged."

"Get *you* discouraged!"

"I backed Jack Wernick's opponent in the last election. Jack's a brilliant man, but he just wants to use Sewanka as a stepping-stone. And he holds grudges."

"Great," I said. "Then this case is tailor-made for him. He can prosecute a big, headline-grabbing case. If he wins, he gets the backing of the rich and powerful Mr. Whitten. And the satisfaction of having pushed your nose in in the process."

"That's right. And, Matt, I don't see how he can fail to win, as things stand now. They can put Dan right inside the house. Angry. He broke those banister posts. There were microscopic splinters in the creases of his hands. Little chips of paint, too. Both matched."

I could see now why she'd been inside so long. They kept her around to taunt her with all these test results.

"I still think he's innocent."

Eve took my hand this time. She spoke to me as she might to a three-year-old. "Matt, you're a good friend. But it's a matter of a few years versus his whole *life*. Don't you owe it to him to talk some sense into him?"

I have never been more confused. Everything Eve said made things look worse. Yet Dan had been surprised, dammit. I *knew* him. Then again, I'd thought I'd known people before . . .

"All right, God damn it, all right." I rubbed my eyes. "When do I see hm?"

"He's being arraigned tomorrow morning—"

"This morning?"

"That's right!"

"They're not wasting any time, are they?"

"Why should they?" I didn't have an answer for that, so Eve went on. "Anyway, I'll arrange for you to talk to him right after they bring him to the other jail. Meanwhile, I'll sound Wernick out about the deal."

"All right," I said, then swore. I pulled out my wallet and threw some money on the table. "Let's get out of here," I said.

"You didn't finish your breakfast."

I looked at her and tried to decide whether to laugh or cry. It was a draw. My face felt dead. I told Eve I'd ordered too heavy a breakfast anyway. We shook hands outside. She went to her office; I went back to the Sewanka Inn and tried to care about cable TV franchises.

CHAPTER 13

"Welcome to Fantasy Island!"
—Ricardo Montalban, "Fantasy Island" (ABC)

I gave up on the hearing after twenty minutes. I went up to my room, took a shower to wash the night off me, and went to bed. I slept surprisingly well; I dropped right off and had no nightmares, about Spot or anything else. It lasted about an hour and forty minutes.

The phone rang. I grabbed it, and in the half-second or so between the time I took it off the cradle and the time I brought it to my ear, all sorts of wonderful scenarios dashed through my brain. Debbie wasn't really dead. The police had caught a mad karate expert who had escaped from an institution to terrorize the countryside. Spot had developed the power of speech (shades of my nightmare) and provided eyewitness testimony that somebody else—like Grant Sewall or somebody—had done Debbie in.

No such luck. The caller was Hans, from the restaurant. He was in tears.

"What's the matter, Hans?"

"The police are coming. They have said they want to come to talk to me about the murder of Daniel's young lady."

"Routine. I told him we'd had a talk there. They'll just want to see if you can confirm it."

"What should I *tell* them, though?"

"The truth, Hans. Just tell them the truth."

"Everything? Even what I later overheard?"

"What's that, Hans?"

"I am walking around, making sure everything is okay. I hear Daniel say, 'If I must strangle her, this wedding will I stop!' Do you want me to tell this to the police? If you say so, I will not tell them. If they ask me, I will lie."

I didn't say anything. Hans said, "Matthew, what should I do?"

I looked at the ceiling. I remembered once in kindergarten, at report-card time, the teacher wrote in the teacher's comments, "Matthew is a very responsible child." I asked my parents what it meant. My father, a renowned wit, said, "It means when anything goes wrong, you're responsible." Everybody laughed, and I got indignant until matters were explained to me. Then I laughed, too. I was beginning to think, though, that what my father said was more a prophecy than a joke.

Why does it always fall to *me* to make these goddam decisions? I asked the universe. The universe told me to shut up and get on with it.

If Hans lied, the police would be denied another incriminating fact. I mean, Dan was only using a figure of speech, but by the time the DA got through with it, it would sound like Dan had signed a confession in triplicate. So it would be nice to keep that out of their hands.

On the other hand, if they found out *anyway*, not only would Dan be in deep yogurt, Hans and I would be there along with him. I wasn't crazy about the idea of going to jail, and I was even less crazy about sending old Hans there, just for incriminating a good friend.

Still, if I said it was okay, Hans would go out there and

lay the foundation for a charge of premeditation. Of course, we were going to plea-bargain away from all of that. I snorted. "*We.*"

No. Couldn't risk it. "Tell them the truth, Hans," I told him. "Anything they ask you."

"Are you sure?"

"Don't keep asking me that. Yes, I'm sure," I lied.

Hans bubbled over again. "If only he'd listened to me," he sobbed. "Forget about her, that's what he should have done."

It was depressing to realize that despite his obviously genuine concern, Hans had no doubt whatever that Dan was guilty. I sighed and thanked him and hung up.

As soon as I did, the phone rang again. It was my wakeup call. It was time to go to the jail and talk to my friend and convince him to stand up in court and say he killed the woman he loved.

Dan was no longer in the local lockup. He'd been transferred sometime before sunrise to the county penitentiary, a yellow brick building outside of town. It looked like a small electronics factory or maybe a junior high school, except maybe for the armed guards.

Eve had supposedly cleared the way for my appearance with those who had to approve, but I was still a good half hour being frisked, questioned, checked, and generally intimidated.

Finally, I was led to the visitors' room, something like the lobby of an unsuccessful bank. The thick Plexiglas windows looked like tellers' cages, and the guards looked like bank guards everywhere, only more bored.

I sat down on a little stool in front of one of the windows and waited. Two guards led Dan to the window. He was manacled. No one, it seemed, was taking any chances with the Mad Karate Killer.

Dan showed me a crooked smile as he sat and picked up

his telephone receiver. I picked up my own and got on with things.

"Another fine mess I've gotten me into," he said.

I wanted to tell him to knock off the macho bullshit, but after a moment's consideration, I decided it might not be such bullshit after all. Dan had gone through a lot during the last couple of days. The least I could do was let him hold on to his courage.

"We've got good people working on it," I told him.

"The lady lawyer?"

"Yes. And anybody else we need to get."

"Like who?"

"Lab experts. Private eyes. Doctors—"

The phone made his voice tinny and filtered some of the emotion from it. Some. Not nearly enough to hide the scorn when he said, "Doctors?"

Dan grabbed a bearded cheek with one strong hand and made a fist, twisting his handsome face into a passable imitation of the Horrible Melting Man. He squeezed hard and kept it up for a good five seconds. It hurt just to look at him. I couldn't even tell him to stop because he had the phone away from his ear.

At last he let go and talked to me again. "Your lawyer friend," he said slowly, "thinks I killed Debbie."

"She doesn't. It doesn't matter what she th—"

"*She wants me to plead guilty!*" He hissed it.

"She's trying to do her best for you. Have you considered the alternatives, Dan?"

Dan's face died. The only signs of life in it at all were the red marks where he'd squeezed it. He looked at me that way for ten seconds. Long, miserable seconds. At last, I looked away.

"You too, Matt? Of all people? Want me to take the easy way? What happened? Your job finally corrupted you? It's funny. I would have said it was impossible. Of course, I would have said a lot of things were impossible."

"Dan," I said, "we're talking about the rest of your *life*."

"I'm innocent"—he'd started shouting; the guard took a step toward him, and his voice dropped to a whisper—"*I'm innocent, you stupid son of bitch!* And I *have* considered the alternatives. Let me tell you, Matt, in a world where Debbie's been murdered and you've sold me out, prison doesn't seem all that bad. Except for one thing. If I get this hung around my neck, the guy who killed Debbie is going to get away with it."

Dan hung up the phone and turned around to call for the guard to take him away. I couldn't let that happen yet, so I gave the glass an open-palmed smack that rattled it like a basketball backboard. Dan picked up the phone again.

"All right," I told him. "You're the boss. If money, brains, and perseverance can get you loose, you will be gotten loose. I'm proud of you, Dan. I think you're a horse's ass, but I'm proud of you."

"Why am I a horse's ass? Because I want to fight for my name?"

"No, because you're going to trust my brain to figure a way to do it."

"Yeah," he said. "After this bullshit this afternoon, I think you've got a point."

I called him a name, and we laughed. Then the laughter stopped, and Dan began to weep. It was something I'd never seen before. Tears rolled down his face and wet his beard. "I didn't kill her, Matt, I swear. I couldn't kill her. I loved her. You've got to help me."

And so on. "You've got it, partner," I told him. "I promise. Listen. I'm going to try to come back here later, with Eve Bowen; maybe I can talk to you in person. If I can't, you'll talk to her, but in either case, I want you to think about everything that happened the other night. Every single thing. I need whatever I can get—"

"There *is* something!" Dan said. "I thought you knew it, but I guess not. It probably won't do any good anyway."

I was about to tell him to let me worry about that but was interrupted by a hand on my shoulder. Mr. Outside. He said, "Time's up."

I wanted to shove him away and berate him for interrupting an important conversation, but reason prevailed. I couldn't do Dan much good if I was in jail, too. I'd get the news later.

I told Dan to keep fighting, then allowed Mr. Outside to show me the door.

Just before I left, I looked back over my shoulder where Dan's guard was adjusting the manacles. Dan managed to raise a hand enough to give me a thumbs-up signal.

His faith, I thought, was touching. It's always nice to have something to live up to. I left the building and went to meet Eve. I was interested to see how she'd react to the news that any deal she'd managed to cook up with the DA was off.

CHAPTER 14

"Make sure you are right; then go ahead."
—Fess Parker, "Disneyland" (ABC)

Eve caught up with me at her office; I was just hanging up the phone as she walked in. "I hope you don't mind," I told her. "Long-distance call. Your secretary said it would be all right."

She looked angry, but she said, "Of course it's all right. Whom did you call?"

"The Network. I was quitting my job, so I didn't think it was right to call collect."

Eve looked at me as if I were crazy. "You quit your job?"

"Yes. I'm damned if I'm going to worry about some stupid cable TV franchise while this is going on."

"This? What is *this?*"

"The case, Eve. I'm going to have to devote full time to it. Your client has decided he doesn't want any part of a deal with the DA. He'll tell you so himself, when he gets the chance."

"Get out of my chair."

"Oh. Sorry." I stood up and walked around her desk to the visitor's chair. Eve put some papers down, sat in her own chair, and closed her eyes. She tented her fingers in her lap, let out a big sigh—in short, did the whole harried-executive number. Eyes still closed, she said, "No deal, then."

"He wants to fight it out," I said. "And, to tell you the truth, I'm glad of it."

She opened her eyes to slits and looked at me disdainfully. "You would," she said. "Well, my father used to say everything works out for the best. This is just more evidence for him." She brushed some red hair from her eyes. "The DA wants to fight it out, too, Matt. He won't be a part of a deal either. Won't even talk about it. Do you know what that means?"

"He's very confident of his case."

"That's the least of it, Matt. I've plea-bargained cases where the defendant was caught red-handed, then signed confessions. In triplicate. No, what this really means is that Jack Wernick is determined to please Mr. Whitten with a revenge show. He's going to try to destroy Dan, not just convict him." She said something libelous about the district attorney.

"So we fight," I said.

"Yes, Matt, we fight. I hope Dan is happy with the results." She started to laugh, ironic laughter that made her face look suddenly cruel.

"What's so funny?" I demanded.

"It all depends now, doesn't it?"

"On what?"

"On how good I am at being a hypocrite."

The humor escaped me. "How many times do I have to apologize for that? What do we do now?"

"*I* confer with my client. I don't know what *you* think you're doing. You may be paying me, but you are likely to be a prosecution witness. I may even have to use you as an alternative suspect to my client."

I shrugged. "Go right ahead. I've been accused of murder before." She gave me a skeptical look. "The next time you come to New York, I'll show you newspapers. But yes, go ahead and pin it on me if it will help. I'll tell you how it could have happened. Debbie slips on the carpet in the upstairs hall, hits herself across the throat on the banister, giving her that bruise and knocking the wind out of her. Brenda and Spot arrive. Spot goes to Debbie and for some reason licks that makeup off her face, while Brenda starts to scream. I arrive, rush to Debbie, and kneel by her side. I distract Brenda's attention somehow and finish Debbie off with one good shot to the larynx."

Eve smiled at me. "You still have the knack, don't you? Do go on, Matt. Just as a forensic exercise, of course. What's your motive?"

"Take your pick. Jealousy. I've secretly been in love with Debbie all these years, but she's been so busy with these two other guys she never notices me, and I can't take it anymore. Jealousy again, over her riches, this time. It's a political murder. Off the pigs and like that."

Eve nodded. "Or how about righteous anger? This woman was a continuing blight on your best friend's existence. Someone had to find a way to make her stop being one."

I nodded ruefully. "You've pegged my feelings precisely, except for the fact that my idea of stopping her did not include murder."

"You didn't kill her, Matt, more's the pity." She picked up one of the papers she'd brought in. "At least you didn't do it the way you've suggested." She handed it to me. "This is the medical examiner's report. One blow, Matt."

I held it a second without opening it. "Before I look, how about the rest of it? Could it have been an accident? The banister?"

Eve shook her head. "Read the report. You'll see." I started to read. After a few seconds, Eve said, "I don't know why I'm letting you do this."

"I'll tell you in a minute," I murmured and went on with the report.

It started with general stuff—Caucasian female, age, height, weight, good general health, like that. I skimmed over it until I got to the cause of death. Eve was right. The banister was out. It was too wide and too hard to have caused the bruise on Debbie's throat. It couldn't have even been the edge of the railing that did it. Debbie had been struck with something rounded. The medical examiner said the facts suggested very strongly that she had been struck by something that had a hard core surrounded by padding. Something, he hardly needed to add, very much like the edge of a hand. The edge of a karate expert's hand.

The ME must have known something about karate himself or he'd swotted up on it for this report, because he went on to detail possibilities. The blow had been delivered from directly in front of Debbie or so close as to make no difference. It took her up under the right side of the jaw and ran diagonally downward. The main force of the blow was concentrated on Debbie's larynx, which was crushed. The ME said this meant that the killer was right-handed or at least struck with the right hand, a backhanded chop that no one could have survived—it not only crushed her larynx but ruptured the carotid artery. She died, the report said, in seconds.

I shuddered. Eve wanted to know what the matter was.

"Says here she died in seconds. Doesn't say how many, but I'm sure it was long enough. I got a flash of what must have been going through Debbie's mind during those seconds. The pain. The inability to breathe. The shock that someone would *do* this to her. It was all in the look on her face when I found her."

"That's great, Matt. Write it down and give it to Wernick. He'll use the same image when he sums up for the jury; he just won't say it as well." There was distaste in her voice and something like pity, but it was cold, detached.

"Well, that is the professional attitude, I guess."

"That's right," she said sourly. "It is. I have no time to sympathize with the victim. Professionally, that is. I have to concentrate on my client. How long do you think I would last as a criminal lawyer if I let my imagination run away with me like that?"

"It's going to take some imagination to figure out what's really going on here. Assuming, as I do, your client is innocent."

"That's what we're forced to assume," she conceded.

"Won't that be jolly for us when we prove he is."

She nodded, her lips tight together. "You go right ahead and prove it, Matt. I'm behind you all the way. Use your imagination and whatever else it takes.

"Because you got me into this. I know how your brain works, how quickly and creatively you think. It's hopeless, but if I'm going to be able to do *anything* for this man, I need you."

She wasn't cold and detached now. I told her she had me, then I finished reading the report. There wasn't much to it.

We discussed ways of getting me in to talk to Dan. The first thing she decided to do was to have me placed under subpoena as a *defense* witness. Then she made a few phone calls. In a spare moment, she covered the receiver and told me to get lost because she'd have no time for lunch. I was to meet her at the jail, and we'd see how she'd done.

I got up, walked around the desk, took her hand, and mouthed,"Thank you."

Eve smiled. It was a weary smile but a warm one, and her hand was warm; and, in spite of everything, I felt better than I had in days.

CHAPTER 15

*"Son, never in the history of American Show
Business has the U.S. Cavalry arrived too late!"*
—Moe Howard, "The Three Stooges" (Syndicated)

The feeling didn't last too long. Dan's big news turned out
to be that he had seen a car driving away just as he'd gone
into the house. Now, the fact that somebody else was on the
grounds that night was good news, and the fact that Dan was
fairly certain the car was Grant Sewall's Mercedes made it
even better. But it didn't do much, if anything, toward
clearing Dan or even toward pointing a suspicious finger at
Grant.

For one thing, Dan saw the car *leaving* as he went inside;
by his own testimony, Debbie had been alive then. Dan's
whole problem was to get someone to believe she'd still
been alive when he himself had left, about seven minutes
later.

That was another problem. Sure, Grant may have come
back yet again, but that would have meant he'd returned,
gone inside, killed his fiancée, left, and gotten completely
out of sight before Brenda returned. Not much time for that.
Still, it was a crumb. I'd have to talk to both of them.

Dan had been glad to see the car. "I figured he came back
to try to make up and failed. Debbie wouldn't admit it, but

she was agitated. I figured she was about ready to listen to reason. That's why I was so upset on the way out and punched those posts out of the railing." Then he started to cloud up again. His lawyer, probably used to this sort of thing, looked up into the corner of the cell as if her schedule for the rest of the day had been written up there.

I wasn't used to seeing my best friend go to pieces, and I hated it. I was about ready to start crying with him. Dan must have noticed, because he shook it off—just closed his eyes tight and shook his head the way Spot does when he steps out of the water. Dan's face folded into a sad-eyed smile.

"Okay, everybody. Get to work on this. I'd help you if I could. Honest."

Eve called the guard, and we went to work. Or she did. I went to the Sewanka Inn to check out. I'd quit the Network; I couldn't go on letting them pay for my lodging, not that they would. To make it easier for the accounting of all concerned, I moved into Dan's apartment on the north side of town.

God, apparently, was paying close attention to the proceedings here, because a dark, featureless overcast had rolled in while Eve and I were talking to Dan. Appropriate stage setting. I couldn't help noticing it because Dan's apartment was mostly windows. It was a garden apartment, second floor, in a development of several hundred units. Dan kept it neat. He had a bedroom, a long room that he had divided into an office (with his new Apple III computer), and a *dojo*, with a mat for his karate practice. It was as bare and Spartan as the inside of a refrigerator. Especially the inside of *Dan's* refrigerator, which had some bean sprouts and some plain yogurt, along with two onions. I could eat that stuff, I suppose, but not frequently. There was nothing to give Spot, either.

Spot. He had to leave the Whittens', that was obvious. It

would give me a good reason to go out there and ask some questions, too. Still, I was having trouble working up enthusiasm for the project. It's a conflict I frequently have with myself. My brain is constantly coming up with ideas I'd rather believe I'm too nice to think of.

That's what was going on now. I'd been exercising some logic; it was enough to make me swear off logic. Eventually, I swore at the room and the world at large, picked up the phone, and dialed the Whitten residence. The maid answered. I gave a phony name and asked for Miss Brenda Whitten. When I was told Miss Whitten was not at home, I was happy.

For a few seconds. Then I realized they were screening the calls. Every newsman in the free world, and at least one from TASS, was probably trying to interview the Whittens. Not even a newspaper magnate's family was going to put up with that.

There was no way around it. I was going to have to go out there in person and take my chances.

But not quite yet. I had to do some boning up first. I pulled down a book from the shelves in Dan's bedroom. *Karate: Body and Balance* by Henry Norman, a good Japanese name if I ever heard one. The sky made it too dark to read without lights, and I was tired of looking at grayness anyway, so I pulled down the shades and sat in a basket chair under a lamp and began to read.

I'm a good reader (not always true of an English major, by the way), but the book was tough going for a while. It assumed a greater knowledge of the martial arts than I possessed, so I had to stop and visualize things frequently.

I'd gotten things fairly well worked out when the phone rang.

"Matt?" It was Brenda Whitten. She was putting a heartiness into her voice that she didn't feel.

"Hello, Brenda," I said quietly. "I tried to call you before."

"So that *was* you. I thought it was. Daddy had forbidden me to speak to you or that lawyer, but to hell with him. I called her to find out where you were. Matt, I have to talk to you. Can you come out here?"

"Sure. But wouldn't it be better to meet somewhere? What about your father?"

"I can't leave here. Besides, you've got an excuse—you'll be coming to pick up Spot."

I smiled. "Great minds run in similar channels," I said.

"What?" I told her never mind. "Okay, Matt," she went on. "Anyway, don't worry about my father. He's such a wreck, the doctor's given him a sleeping pill. He'll be out for hours. Please come."

I told her I would. I was about to hang up when Brenda spoke again. "Matt?"

"Yes, Punkin?" I was astonished to hear myself call her that—that was Dan's pet name for her.

Brenda didn't seem to notice. "It's a mess, isn't it, Matt?" I remember thinking it should be illegal for a little girl to sound that sad.

Spot has been known to punish me for ignoring him, and God knows I'd been ignoring him, but this time he showed nothing but gladness at the sight of me. Everybody who lives in close proximity to an animal tends to anthropomorphize. I knew Spot wasn't making allowances because I was so depressed; I just wanted to believe he was because I felt better that way. I took some time and showed my appreciation, scratching him under the chin and behind the ears. Spot closed his eyes and enjoyed it.

Then I found out why he was in such a good mood. "I mated him to Vanilla today."

"Oh," I said. So he'd had his little canine ashes hauled, had he? "What did your father say about that?"

"He doesn't know. And I don't care if he finds out, either. It—it was something Debbie wanted." She was silent for a second. "So I took care of it. Let's take a walk, Matt."

"It's going to rain."

"We won't go far. Just halfway around the house. Spot could use the exercise, and there are plenty of doors we can duck into if it starts to rain. Besides, I want to practice walking." She grinned and held her hands out to her sides. "See? No crutches!"

"Wow, I *have* been preoccupied. That's great, Junebug. How long have you been going without them?"

"Just since this morning, but I think it's going to be easy."

"Don't overdo it, now."

"Piece of cake, Matt, honest. My hip is a little sore from dragging the thing"—she knocked on the artificial leg through her jeans—"but I've got to build up the muscles anyway. Come on, Matt. I'm bringing you along to carry me if anything goes wrong."

I laughed. "Only a knave could resist the plea of a damsel in distress."

We left the house. I had to help her down the front stoop, but once we hit the walkway, she was on her own. She had a decided limp, of course, and when she tried to go too fast, she had trouble keeping her balance, but other than that, she got along fine.

Spot was happy, too. He danced along, yipping, chasing odd bits of things that were blown along by the pre-shower breeze.

Brenda said, "I'm going to miss Dan, Matt. I hate this."

"He's not gone yet, Brenda."

"Oh, but the *evidence*. I heard my father talking to the district attorney—"

"That figures."

"—and it—well, it sounds like poor Dan doesn't have a chance."

"Poor Dan," I thought. That was interesting. After all, to the best of her knowledge and belief, "Poor Dan" had killed her sister. I toned that down some and mentioned it to Brenda.

Brenda looked miserable. "Oh, God, Matt, I know. I'm all mixed up. I can't eat, I can't sleep—I hate it that this has happened, but sometimes . . ."

The wind picked up. The new leaves on the trees made a noise like fire.

"Look, Matt," she went on. "Have you ever loved someone you didn't like?"

The question stopped me in my tracks. Dan had said almost the same thing, that night at the House of Hans. I simply said yes.

"Okay, then," Brenda said. She stood facing me. "Then you know how I felt about Debbie. She was beautiful and smart and basically a good person. Really . . . but she *wasted* it. Dan was right about her, you know. She—she—"

"It doesn't matter now, Junebug." I shook my head. "That's not right. I meant to say, whatever the case, she deserved better than she got."

Brenda smiled through tears. "The Old Professor strikes again. You even correct your own grammar, don't you?"

"We strive for precision," I told her.

"Okay. But it's hard to say precisely what I'm trying to say." The wind pushed a strand of her hair across her face and held it there; she brushed it away. "I—well, I miss my sister, and I want her back—but sometimes I think about Dan and what he went through for her, and I think he *should* have killed her. He should have killed her! Sometimes, I want to just scream!"

I told her I knew the feeling.

She turned her pretty face to me. It was very serious, very earnest. "Matt, you have to get Dan out of this somehow. You have to. Whatever he did, he doesn't deserve to rot in jail for it."

I looked at her, into her round blue eyes, and had a thought, a thought I hated myself for. But of course I followed up on it; I'm not even surprised anymore at what I'm capable of.

"You can help, Brenda," I said, "if you want to."

"Name it, Matt. Bring me to that lady lawyer. Just tell me what to say."

"That won't be necessary," I snapped. I was getting a little tired of people volunteering to perjure themselves if I would speak but the word.

"Okay, then, how can I help?" She put a hand on my arm. "I'm sorry, Matt."

I let go some air and relaxed a little. "Me too. Like I said, I've been preoccupied." I patted her hand, and she took it back. "There are two things you can do for me. First, I've got to talk to Grant."

"Yeah?" Brenda said. Her tone said go on.

"Well, I hardly think he's going to want to see me. He's probably going right along with your father on that."

"Okay, I'll arrange it."

"I'm going to say some things he's not going to like," I warned.

"I'll take care of it," she said. "The funeral is tomorrow; he'll be with us all day. I'll think of a place and see that he meets you there. Will you still be at Dan's apartment?"

I told her I would, adding that she should leave a message

at Eve Bowen's office if for any reason I wasn't home. I'd check in with Eve at frequent intervals.

Brenda nodded. "What's the other thing?"

"It's a little ghoulish."

"I expect that from you. What is it?"

"I want you to hit me." There it was.

"What?"

"I want you to hit me." Brenda asked why; I made up some plausible-sounding lie about getting the mechanics of the whole thing nailed down in my mind. Brenda said she thought it was a waste of time but agreed to go along with it.

"Okay," she said, "how should I go about this?" I showed her, roughly, the two possible ways the medical examiner said the karate blow must have been delivered.

"Don't hold back," I told her. "I'm ready for you. If I don't duck, it's my own tough luck."

She tried a few tentative swipes. "This is ridiculous, Matt. I can't shift my weight behind a blow like that, not on this leg."

"Try anyway." We moved off the walkway a few steps onto the soft grass, and she gave it a try. As she'd warned, standing square to me that way and swinging hard and not sideways, as she did to hit a baseball, she overbalanced and fell.

I blocked the blow by catching her arm. It was a powerful blow—Brenda was a strong girl through the arms and shoulders, remember—but nothing like the shot that had killed her sister. Still, it had enough momentum to knock me off my own feet, and we fell to the lawn with Brenda somewhat cushioned by my body.

Brenda began to laugh. "There, you big dummy, what did you learn from *that?*"

I laughed, too, with relief. "I learned I'm a big dummy, what else?" Spot, who had gotten bored with our conversation and wandered off somewhere, now came bounding back to us, yipping happily, eager to join the fun. He jumped on each of us in turn and started licking our faces.

I stopped laughing. I had a sudden flash of Spot licking Debbie Whitten's dead face, and the fun was suddenly gone. I helped Brenda to her feet, and we ended our walk at the back door of the Whitten mansion.

"Made it," she said. She looked proud.

"Well done," I told her. I went into my Oral Roberts impersonation—"In the name of *Jesus,* throw your crutches away."

Brenda smiled but didn't laugh. "Soon, Matt. As soon as I can. I hate them so much. If you only knew..."

"Sure, Junebug," I said. I kissed her good-bye. It was much more of a kiss than I'd expected. I smiled at her. "This little girl is growing up," I said.

"Good of you to notice."

The sky was darker, the wind was stronger, and there was a faint sound of distant thunder when I got back to the car, but I decided to press my luck. I knew from experience that the Sewanka skies could do this for hours before it actually rained. Or it might go on for days and never get around to raining. I still needed groceries, so I drove to a supermarket, locked Spot in the car, dashed inside, and bought three bags' worth of stuff.

I almost made it. I had just pulled into Dan's space in the parking lot when it started to pour. Spot gave me a dirty look as I let him out of the car, then dashed for the cover of the entranceway, leaving me to deal with the groceries.

I was soaked before I went ten steps, and worse than that, the bags were getting soaked. It was the kind of situation I hate, the kind that can ruin a whole day, and my days lately didn't take a whole lot of ruining. All I could do was run blindly for the entrance and hope the bags wouldn't give way, even though I could feel them going.

Suddenly, an umbrella was held over my head, and someone said, "Can I help you with that?" and one of the bags was taken from me, allowing me to regrasp the other two and support their soggy bottoms. I looked up to see who my benefactors were, and what to my wondering eyes should appear but Harris Brophy and Shirley Arnstein.

Harris's self-confident grin shone brightly even in the downpour. "Relax, Matt. The cavalry has arrived."

CHAPTER 16

*"Let's check the scores at halftime and see
where we stand."*
—Robert Earle, "G.E. College Bowl" (NBC)

At Shirley's command, Harris would tell me nothing until I
got out of those wet clothes and took a shower before I
caught cold. Fair enough. I was already beginning to sneeze.
Still, it was one of my quickest showers—three minutes,
tops, and another two to dry off and dress.

I was still wiping my hair when I rejoined the gang.
"Okay, now talk. What are you two doing up here?"

"Snatching a weekend of bliss at the Network's expense,"
Harris said.

Shirley blushed bright red. Shirley Arnstein was plain but
pleasant-looking. She was very shy, except when it came to
her job. She was a compulsive worker, the kind, frankly,
that gets taken advantage of. People will leave things unfinished because someone like Shirley will come along and
take care of them because they need to be done. Right now,
for example, she was drying Spot. She was also very much
in love with Harris Brophy, something he seemed to take for
granted. It was uncertain how Harris felt about Shirley, because it was uncertain how he felt about anything.

"Ha, ha," I said. "Come on, Harris. Who's watching the Network?"

He raised his eyebrows. "What do you care? You've quit, remember?"

He was absolutely right, but I was not in the mood to be put down. I told him so, and said they might as well get back to the hotel and get on with the bliss.

"Relax, Matt," Shirley said. She was rubbing vigorously at Spot's neck. She finished with him, brought the towel to the hamper, then came back and looked around the room, as though planning to start dusting next. "Harris was only kidding," she said.

"We came to get the Network car," Harris said. "Didn't it occur to you when you called me to resign that you no longer had the right to drive it?"

I sat there and shook my head. "No, it didn't." I wasn't going to be able to do Dan a bit of good if I didn't get my brain together very soon. "But it doesn't take two of you to get the car, does it?"

"No, but the Network needs someone at these hearings, especially now. Shirley, tell him about it."

Now she had something to do, so she could stop fidgeting. "Well, Marty Adelman is going to be okay. He regained consciousness last night, and I went to speak to him. He confirms that the man you met up here, Roger Sparn, the ComCab representative, came to visit him a few weeks ago, trying to get the Network to ease up on his company. Marty says he implied that if they just left ComCab alone for a year or so, they could come to some sort of an arrangement about Network Cable Arts."

"What kind of an arrangement?"

"Marty says he didn't get specific. That note in his pocket, by the way, was to remind him to call you and tell you about Sparn."

"Well," I said, "it's confirmation of what you already

know, but it's just about the way I figured things were when I first heard about the visit."

Still, it was disappointing that Marty's news wasn't as important as the note seemed to promise, and it rankled that Sparn had felt obligated to mention the visit minutes before I found out about Marty's "accident." I tried to figure what it might mean, some kind of angle . . .

"What am I doing?" I snapped. "Look, Harris, Shirley, I don't have time for this. I've got to work on my own case."

Harris was chuckling. I stared at him. My arms went tight with the effort to stop myself form smashing his handsome grin against the back of his head.

"Harris," I said, "I used to put up with a lot of bullshit from you because I was your boss and you were the best in the industry at what you do. I needed you. I don't need you anymore. The fact that my best friend is accused of murder is not to be laughed at. Is that clear? If you ever make any friends, you might understand."

Harris's grin never wavered, but the happy gleam left his eyes for a split second, then returned. "Sure, Matt," he said quietly. "No offense meant."

"All right, then. But really, I'm tired, and I've got a lot of work to do, so if you don't mind . . ." I reached into my pocket and got the keys to the Network car. I held them out to him, but he wouldn't take them.

"Keep them," Harris said. "You'll need something to get around in, and I'll be dipped in the Gowanus Canal before I let you drive Trigger."

Trigger was Harris's pride and joy, a 1959 Plymouth in white and gold, like a palomino, hence the name. He kept it in perfect condition and had once turned down an offer of fifteen thousand dollars for it.

I was incredulous. "You drove Trigger up here?"

"Sure, I like to get the old stallion on the highway every once in a while. What power. What acceleration."

"We could pass everything on the road coming up but the gas stations," Shirley chimed in. "But Harris, we haven't told Matt the important part yet."

"No, we haven't. Matt, the reason both of us came upstate is that ComCab is going to take some looking into. Shirley is going to stay around Sewanka, and I'll be going on to a little town outside Rochester where they have their headquarters.

"But even working in New York, I found something I think you're going to find very interesting. I got it from my top Wall Street source." Harris Brophy's sources tended to be attractive secretaries. "It was a proposed stock deal. Big minority interest in ComCab, something like twenty-three per cent, was earmarked for sale to a buyer here in Sewanka."

I raised a brow. That was interesting. "Whitten Communications?" I guessed.

Harris grinned again, but this time I didn't mind at all. "Close. Mr. Grant Sewall. In his own person. As an individual."

I rubbed my jaw, thinking about it. "Why didn't it go through?"

"My source couldn't tell me. She seemed—" I thought I caught a brief flash of discomfort on Shirley's face at the word "she." Harris must have seen it, too, because he started over. "My source seemed to think Sewall was going to get the presidency of the company as soon as the deal was complete."

"When was this?"

"About two years ago. This any help, Matt?"

I was thinking. Two years, hmm. "It just might be, Harris. Thanks. Thanks, Shirley."

"I figured you'd like it," he said.

"Why's that?"

"Well, before we left, Shirley did a quick job of research on everything that's been printed about the case."

"I don't think I missed anything," Shirley said proudly.

"I'm sure you didn't," I told her.

"We talked it over in the car on the way up. Now, taking it for granted that your friend is clean—"

"Watch it, Harris."

Harris came as close to getting angry then as anyone has ever seen him. "Lighten up, Matt. I *said* we were taking it for granted. So, if your friend is clean, the killer either had to be you, which is unlikely, unless you have some *beaucoup* special motive. It would take a dilly to make a murderer out of a nice guy like Matt Cobb, and I haven't been able to think of one."

"Thank you, I think."

Harris ignored it. "It either had to be you, or it had to be the old man—"

"Impossible. I was with him the whole time, except for a minute or so, and he couldn't have done it in that time unless he took a rocket to the house and back."

"All right, then. The papers weren't absolutely clear on that." Shirley sounded almost apologetic.

"Besides," I added, "what motive did he have?"

Harris shrugged. "I'm just running down possibilities. How about the girl?"

"Brenda? No."

"Don't tell me it hadn't crossed your mind. She *was* the first one back to the house."

"Oh, it crossed my mind, all right." For which God help me, I thought. "I even tested it out this afternoon. It's no good. Even if she knew anything about karate, which she doesn't, she just couldn't have delivered that blow the way the ME says it was delivered. She can't be fluid enough on the artificial leg to get her body behind it, and she doesn't have enough upper-body strength to come close to doing it on arms alone. I saw her; I'm sure of it. Besides, she doesn't have a motive either."

"An outsider doesn't look likely," Harris said. "Even *you* have to admit that."

I thought that one over. It was interesting because of what we knew about Grant. Assuming Grant's innocence for the sake of the outsider theory, we knew it *couldn't* have been an outsider because Grant would have seen him as he was leaving the estate himself. Of course, someone else could have been using Grant's car, but I could check that tomorrow.

There were a *lot* of things for me to check on Saturday. I was looking forward to my talk with Grant with more enthusiasm all the time. As Harris put it just before he and Shirley left to go to dinner, "From your point of view, Matt, I don't think you can let the killer be anybody *but* Mr. Grant Sewall."

CHAPTER 17

"...and don't forget to say your prayers."
—Bob Keeshan, "Captain Kangaroo" (CBS)

The sun was out Saturday morning, but the ground was still wet from yesterday's soaking rain. The lush green of Saint Elizabeth's Cemetery was soft and slippery, and before long began to show little curves of brown where the feet of mourners had broken through the grass.

I stood well back from the grave. I don't like funerals in the first place, and I don't think I would have been welcome at this one. That didn't stop the police, of course. Chief Cooper was there, without a stitch of plaid on him; I didn't know he could do it. He was wearing a very nice navy blue suit, white shirt, black tie. I wondered how he kept it nice in the wild.

The press was there, too, but at a discreet distance. They wanted news. Nothing at all had happened on Friday. I stood among them. Camouflage. We were close enough to hear the eulogy without horning in on the mourners.

Les Tilman spotted me and came over to talk. He whispered quietly while Bishop Peterstone of the Northfield Episcopal Church led prayers for the soul of Debra Whitten.

"You've got a lot of balls, showing up here," Les said conversationally.

I didn't say anything. I couldn't tell him the truth—that Brenda had called this morning and insisted the cemetery was where the meeting with Grant should take place, despite my best efforts to talk her out of it—and I never lie to the press if I can help it.

"Come on, Cobb," the tubby little reporter whispered. "Give me a quote for the afternoon edition."

"That's all I need," I told him. "I suppose there's no chance of your ignoring my being here at all."

He looked up at me with narrowed eyes. "Maybe. Let's take a little walk." We squished across the grass until we came to the white gravel path that ran through the cemetery.

For a full minute, Les devoted his attention to cleaning his shoes. "Damn mud. Soil in this place is like glue when it gets wet. Next time I have to cover a funeral here in spring, I'm going barefoot, so help me."

"What's on your mind, Les?"

There was a look of real pain on his face. It made him look his real age. "You want me to keep you out of the papers. Why?"

"Because it would be embarrassing to the family and to me."

"Okay. But why? Why are you here? Why don't you want me to print you were here?"

"Nice talking to you, Les." I could still see the grave site. They were about finished over there. Mourners were throwing flowers on the coffin. I figured it was about time to head over to my rendezvous point.

Les, with his short legs, had to run on the gravel to catch up with me. "All right, how about if I guess? You're here trying to pick up something that will help your friend. Is that it? Off the record, but I've got to know."

"Yeah, that's it, Les."

"Okay, then. I won't print it. If anybody else spots you, you're on your own, but from me, you're in the clear."

It was my turn to ask why. "Do you have something that will help Dan? Tell me, Les, it's important."

"Nah, I've got nothing. From where I sit, he looks guilty as hell. She broke his heart, and he killed her for it. Simple as that."

"Simple as that? For Christ's sake, Les, if I killed every woman who broke my heart, Playtex would go out of business!"

"I like that," Les said. "But all this isn't the point, is it?"

"It is for me. What the hell are you talking about?"

"Look. I've been in the newspaper business a long time, and I've managed to work myself up to the exalted position of city room hack. I'm the top local newsman in Sewanka, New York, which is like being king of the moon. But that's not the point either.

"The point is *journalism*. I'm in this business to print the truth—laugh at me, and I'll kill you—and that's what I want to print. We're under orders down at the shop. Make it look fair but crucify Morris all the same."

"Yeah," I said, "I've noticed a certain trend in that direction."

"The old man, I could take it from. Sewall, he's got an excuse, too. But the editor down there is just trying to kiss ass. That's his privilege, but he's not going to do it with my lips, if you follow me. *I* may not deserve any respect, but I'm old enough to remember when my profession did.

"So here's the deal. You do what you have to do. I'm going to cover this story fairly if it costs me my job, which it probably will. But when I go, I'll go out with a blaze of glory. However this turns out, when it's all over, I want an interview with you. Exclusive."

"I thought you said he was guilty."

Les shrugged. "Doesn't matter, it's a great story no matter how it turns out. 'Friend Fights to Save Friend.' Succeeds, fails, or vows to go on despite conviction. They'll have to run it, whether they fire me or not. If they don't, the crooked bastards, I'll sell it to a magazine." I thought it over. It didn't take long. I had nothing to lose and neither did Dan. I said sure, and we shook on it.

"Great," Les said. "And remember, I'm not doing it for you, I'm doing it for my own self-respect."

I smiled in spite of myself. "Les, can I quote you?"

He hit himself in the head. "Jesus," he said, "thirty-three years in the newspaper business, and I get caught. No, don't quote me. This is off the record."

We shook on that, too, and I made my way to the stone bench where Brenda had promised she'd be waiting for Grant. I didn't like the setup; if I remembered Saint Elizabeth's correctly, we'd be about twenty-five yards horizontally and six feet vertically from Debbie's body. It was going to be an added strain on what was bound to be an unpleasant conference in the first place, especially if Brenda got Grant to stay the way she said she was going to. She planned to ask him to stay with her so that they could have some time alone with Debbie.

It stank. The whole setup was terrible. Unfortunately, it was the only chance at Mr. Sewall I was likely to get.

They were there, all right, sitting on a curved marble bench with an angel at either end. Brenda wore a black dress, Grant a light gray suit with a mourning band. Brenda called to me.

Grant was not happy to see me, and when Brenda turned to him and said, "You just be quiet and talk to Matt," he turned purple. But he obeyed. Quite a gentleman, I thought. And with a lot of self-control.

"What could you possibly want to say to me, Cobb?" His voice was strangled.

"Just a few questions." I was keeping calm, but I was

watching Grant's hands. They were balled up into tight fists, and God alone knew what was keeping him from trying to use them to make a muffled drumbeat on my face.

"Do the police know you're here?" He tried to make it a threat. "Do they know you're going around asking *questions?*"

"Probably. Nothing they can do about it. I'm assisting Mr. Morris's attorney, for one thing. For another, I'm a citizen of this state; I pay taxes. I can ask anybody any damn question I please, and they can answer it if they're willing to." I looked him in his blue eyes. "Brenda thought you might be willing to, as a favor to her."

"As a favor to Brenda," he said. It was hard to understand him, he was so mad. *"I will not!* My fiancée has just been buried! This was supposed to be our *wedding day!"*

That point had occurred to me yesterday. Harris Brophy had observed that at least the flowers wouldn't go to waste. It hadn't been one of his more endearing moments.

Grant continued to rage. I thought he might be creating a disturbance, but all the other mourners for other decedents were studiously avoiding us. I suppose emotional outbursts are fairly common in cemeteries, even Episcopal ones. Fortunately, the press had left.

". . . And you come here—*here!*—to ask questions, to try to free the man who killed her!" Grant stood up with the last exclamation point and was about to stomp off.

Brenda spoke very softly. "Please, Grant. Talk to Matt. This is a difficult situation for him, too. If Dan is innocent—"

"You know he's not innocent."

"—if he is, you wouldn't want him to be convicted. If he's guilty, just answering Matt's questions won't save him."

He looked at her. He was a lot less purple now, for which I was grateful. I was hoping to hang a murder on the man. I didn't want him to expire from apoplexy before I got the chance.

"I'm sorry, Brenda," he said. "But I just can't."

"Grant," she said. It was extraordinary, but she managed to be sweet and persuasive and at the same time put plenty into her tone that said, "Don't try my patience." "Grant, as a favor to me, won't you? I really think it's the right thing for you to do."

Grant gave her a fearsome look, a look of pure hostility, but he sat. "Make it short, Cobb," he said. "I've got to get back to the house."

I told him it wouldn't take long, but I thought, never underestimate the power of a woman. The woman in question said she would be waiting for us at the car. She picked up her crutches and made her way carefully to the path, after which she carried them. I watched her go, then I asked Grant my first question.

"What did you and Debbie fight about Wednesday night?"

"None of your business."

I sighed. "Don't be difficult, Grant. Did you tell the police?" He nodded. "If you told them, then I'll find out. A legal practice known as discovery. The DA has to share all his evidence with the defense. What did you fight about?"

He sneered at me. A Ken-doll sneer. "It was about you, if you must know."

"That's interesting. Care to elaborate?"

"I just don't like you, Cobb."

"I'm crushed."

"And I didn't like the idea of your spending every spare moment draped all over Debra and the Whitten family. Don't you think I know what you were up to?"

"Tell me," I said. This was fascinating. I keep running into people like this, people who impose whole sets of fantastic motives into the simple actions I perform as I attempt to muddle through my life. "What was I up to, Grant?"

"Don't be smug, Cobb. You were trying to re-create your tight little clique from college days, trying to get Debra back in the habit of thinking of your Jewish friend as her man, instead of me."

"Oh," I said.

"Yes. And that afternoon I told her so. We argued about it. I decided it would be best if I let her cool off for a day or so. And now, thanks to you, the last words we had together were insults."

"Is that why you drove back later? To try to make up with Debbie?"

"Later? What are you talking about?"

It's such a nice feeling when a bluff pays off. Now I was sure Grant had been back on the estate about the time of the murder. He was trying to play things tough, but his shock at hearing the question seemed to shrink him an inch in every dimension.

"You deny you went back?" I was calm, superior.

He gave me what is known in the world of journalism as a non-denial denial: "I don't know what you're talking about."

I pressed my advantage. "So you haven't told the police yet. That's the only way you'd feel safe lying about it to me. Chief Cooper is going to love hearing about this."

Grant said he still didn't know what I was talking about.

I leaned into him, pointed a finger, and said, "Listen, jerk. I didn't quit my job to play games with you. You were *seen*, Grant. Simple as that."

"I—I don't believe you."

It was time for another bluff. "Oh? Shall I call Brenda back and ask her?" Grant's pretty face was starting to crumble. I went on. "No? All right, then. We'll keep talking. Did you and Debbie fight again when you got back to the house?"

"No!" He wiped his forehead with his thumb. "I never went back inside the house at all."

"Why not?"

"As I approached the carport, I saw that you and Morris were still there—I saw your cars. I decided there wasn't any use in trying to patch things up with Debra when the causes of our argument were still there. I just turned around and drove off."

"I see," I said. "That wasn't so bad, now, was it? Of course, if you'd told the police at the time, they could have checked the drive and found a nice smooth set of tire prints showing how you made a U-turn and left without even stopping the car. Now, all the visitors offering condolences will have obliterated them. You probably figured that the police have the killer in custody, so why confuse them, right?"

He nodded. The expression on his face said he was surprised to see me so understanding.

"Well, Grant, I'm afraid we're going to have to confuse them anyway. I'll give you until Monday to tell them about your little visit. Tell you the truth, though, I hope you don't. It will be so much better for Dan if they have to drag it out of you the way I did."

"I'll tell them, damn you."

"Good boy," I told him. "Now let's talk about the other fight."

"What other fight? That silly bit of tension on Tuesday?"

"No. The one two years ago. The one that broke up your engagement to Debbie."

He started to get angry again. "Really, Cobb. What possible difference can that make?"

"You tell me," I said quietly.

He thought over the situation; I could see him hating it. He didn't know how much I already knew, and he had to be wondering what lengths I'd go to get him to come across with the information. I was beginning to wonder about that myself. I tried to imagine limits for my conduct in this case but couldn't. It was an uncomfortable thought.

Grant was biting his lip. I decided to help him along a little. "It had to do with your deal with ComCab, didn't it? You were going to use Debbie's money, if you could talk her into it, to buy a big part of ComCab and go into competition with her father."

Grant pulled himself together, at least externally, to the point where he seemed his old upper-class, superior self. "You do have ways of digging things up, don't you?"

"You bet your ass," I told him. It was a funny thing. The more patrician Grant became, the cruder I wanted to act. "Then I'm right? Good. The only thing that gets me is that you actually thought Debbie would go along with it."

"It made sense from a business point of view," he said. "An important New York broadcast executive like yourself should appreciate that." He was practically urbane by now. "I simply underestimated Debra's devotion to her family."

"So she told you it was all over, never darken her door again, and ran home from her own engagement party. That must have been very embarrassing for you."

"Oh, it was. Especially when she left her sister stranded. I had to take poor Brenda home; after Debra's blowup and my drowning my sorrows, I was hardly in a condition to be driving at all, let alone with a passenger. I had to stop frequently. As Brenda can tell you—or has she already?—I didn't get her home for hours, and that was nearly as great a scandal as the broken engagement."

"Of course, with the wedding off, the deal fell through."

"Of course." Grant was looking at me shrewdly. I decided he'd figured playing along was the quickest way to get rid of me.

"And it was very open-minded of Mr. Whitten to keep you on after all that."

"Oh, it was. But he never knew the reason for our breakup; Debra took it all upon herself. Which made me love her all the more."

I heard gravel crunching from the walkway. I looked past Grant to see Brenda coming back to us, limping along through the dappled sunlight and humming a happy little tune. The little girl had decided my time was about up.

"Made you love her all the more," I repeated. "Even when she turned around and took up with Dan again? Said she was going to marry him?"

Grant grinned. It was a very handsome grin. You couldn't find one thing wrong with it if you looked for a month. The venom was all in his voice.

"No, Cobb. I wasn't worried, not for a second. Your friend didn't have a chance. Debra kept him as a pet, that's all. He gave her the same undifferentiated affection those ridiculous white dogs do. Debra belonged with me, and she knew it, and I knew she knew it. We stick with our own kind, Cobb."

"So do cockroaches," I told him.

Grant kept smiling. "I wouldn't know," he said. "That would seem to fall under the expertise of you and your friend. All I know, Cobb, is that you'll never get that social-climbing little bastard out of this, because he's guilty and you know it. He couldn't face the fact that Debra was through slumming, so he killed her like the hoodlum he is. You deserve each other."

"Remember you said that," I told him. I was grinning now, too. "Keep it fresh in your memory. Because someday, maybe not soon but someday, *this* hoodlum is going to bring it home to you. We guttersnipes have our ways—this civilized air is only a facade. A gentleman like you should know that instinctively, as I'm sure you do. So rest assured, Mr. Sewall, that those words will return to you. In a sandwich."

I brushed my hands together as if I'd touched something dirty. I was still looking at them when I said, "That's all, Grant. You may go."

I got his reactions through sound effects. Dismissed by a guttersnipe! I wasn't going to be allowed to get away with that. I heard him draw in a bushel of air, the better to issue a challenge, and I heard him spring to his feet, the better to sucker-punch me as soon as I stood up. My mouth started to water. As I'd told him already, we guttersnipes have our ways.

But I never got to use them. Brenda was back, and she'd heard the last part of our exchange. I'd been so involved I hadn't even noticed her. Brenda spoke before Grant or I could say anything.

"Yes, Grant," she said. "You may go. Matt will drive me home."

Grant sniffed. "I have you to thank for this."

"You're welcome," she said. "I'll stay with the hoodlum, thank you. His manners are better."

Grant spun on his heel in the mud and left. Brenda asked me if I'd found out anything useful.

"Useful? Too early to tell. I did learn one thing, though. Dan was right. If your sister had married that wimp, she would have been miserable for the rest of her life."

Brenda looked at me with sad eyes. "Take me home, Matt."

On the way, I checked Grant's story about the party with her. "So someone found out the secret of the great fight, eh?" she said. "I never knew. I always thought it was some stupid thing of Debbie's. I never knew Grant was—I felt *sorry* for him." She sat there looking miserable. "Oh, Debbie, I *apologize!*" was all she said for the rest of the trip.

I pretty much got the silent treatment at the end of the

trip, too. I delivered Brenda to her doorstep, handed her her crutches, then looked up to see A. Lawrence Whitten glowering down at me. He walked down the stairs like a hundred-year-old man and slapped me in the face.

"I ought to kill you," he said.

I didn't say anything. I wasn't in the mood for a reconciliation with this old fool, but I wasn't quite ready to punch him out either. Anything in between would have been a waste of time. I just met his glare for a few seconds to show I wasn't intimidated. Then I got in the car and drove away.

And nobody tried to kill me until the next afternoon.

CHAPTER 18

"Now, what do we mean by that?"
"Yeah! Wadda we mean by that?"
—Soupy Sales and Frank Nastasi;
"The Soupy Sales Show" (Syndicated)

I had a lot of trouble sleeping Saturday night, and when I did sleep, I had crazy dreams again, including the one where Spot talks to me, telling me to pay attention to him. He got pretty abusive about it this time around. I was telling him to get off my back when I woke up.

At least I thought I woke up. I opened my eyes to see Spot again, with his bright brown eyes about three and a half inches from my face. It's an interesting experience to awaken from a nightmare to find the subject of the nightmare right there before you. I greeted Sunday morning by saying something like "Arrgh!" I followed that with a moan when I took a look at the clock and saw what time it was.

The real-life Spot was much easier to get along with than the phantasm was, so I tried to get him to tell me what the hell he wanted in the dream. The Samoyed, however, was interested only in going for a walk. I obliged him; it's part of our deal. In fact, I took him for a good, long walk, about a mile and a half to the nearest shopping center, where I got the Sewanka Sunday *Sun* and the New York *Times*. The Whitten case got a lot of space in the *Times;* they're not that big on crime, and they're even less big on out-of-town crime. The angle that got them interested in Dan was the way Mr. Whitten's outlets were covering the story. I took a look at the front page of the *Sun*, and it was like picking up exhibit A. Les Tilman's story was fairly balanced, for which God bless him, but the rest of the coverage was ridiculous. They did everything short of calling Dan a monster, and they could have even gotten away with that, considering the pictures they ran of him.

After a while, I gave up on the papers and gave the TV a try. I was invited to find Jesus on three local stations and five from out of town. Jesus works very hard on Sunday mornings on television. Of course, local stations love these TV evangelists. They take time nobody else wants, they pay full commercial rates, and, best of all, the station gets to log it as "Rel," which means religious programming. It goes over big with the FCC at license-renewal time.

I remember one guy, who looked like Grant Sewall only thirty years older, telling me in a soft drawl to "give all my troubles to Jesus." It sounded like a good idea, and I considered it, but I was brought up to believe in the Lord that helped those who helped themselves. I decided to hold on to my troubles a little longer. No hard feelings.

I was getting silly. I'm a danger to myself and society at large when I get like that. I needed to talk to somebody. Who did I know who'd be up at that hour (quarter to nine) who wasn't at church?

Shirley Arnstein, of course. She'd probably be making the bed in her hotel room because she wasn't happy with the way the maids did it.

She picked up the phone on the first ring. "Hello, Shirley," I said.

"Matt! I'm so glad you called. I was going to wait until ten o'clock and then call you."

"Oh? Anything happening? Did you hear from Harris?"

"Just that he arrived safely in Rochester. But I'm going to be talking with Roger Sparn about the things Harris found out. I thought I'd get your advice on how to handle it."

That was interesting. When she was working for me, she asked for instructions, not advice. I generally asked her what she thought was best, then let her do it.

That's what I did this time. She surprised me by saying, "I think it would be best if we spoke to him together, Matt. If you don't mind."

I thought about it for a second. It made sense. A talk with the former radio actor was on my agenda anyway. Shirley had her case and I had mine, but there was a significant area of overlap. If we took him together, he wouldn't have time to rehearse any answers.

"Brilliant as usual, Ace," I said. "Shall we have breakfast and plot strategy?"

She thought that was a fine idea, so I took Spot for a ride in the car, picked up Shirley at the Sewanka Inn, then drove out to a place on Route 13 that was famous throughout the Southern Tier for its home fried potatoes.

The crowd was made up of truck drivers and college students at the end of all-nighters, and Shirley and I didn't exactly fit in, but it was a friendly place, and the waitress smiled as she led us to a Formica-topped table.

We never did discuss strategy. Shirley dug a spoon into an enormous bowl of oatmeal and said, "You know, Matt, I know you didn't do this on purpose, but you hurt Harris pretty badly the other day."

I sat there with the ketchup bottle in my hand and laughed. "I what? I didn't know he could be hurt."

"Oh, that's just the way he copes. You should know that."

"What did I do? I think you're kidding me."

"You told him if he ever made any friends, then he'd understand how you feel."

"I was upset."

"It was still a cruel thing to say. Harris—he'd never say this himself, you know—but Harris likes to think he *is* your friend. You're the closest thing to a friend he's got."

Jesus, I thought, that isn't very close. "What about you?"

She waved a hand, dismissing herself. "I'm just a girl who loves him. There are lots of those." She looked down at her oatmeal, moved her spoon a little, and looked back up. "Matt, Harris *admires* you. He *envies* you."

I shook my head in disbelief. I'd always envied *him*. For his cool competence. His detachment. His even temper and confidence.

I put the ketchup down. "What could I possibly have that Harris Brophy would be jealous of?"

"You *feel* things, Matt. You care about things. You can still get excited over a matter of right and wrong. And most of all, *you're willing to attempt something important you might fail at*.

"Harris can't do that. His whole life is structured around the idea that *nothing* is important, so it doesn't matter what he does."

"He doesn't know when he's well off," I said.

"Or you don't. All I'm asking is for you not to throw it up in his face anymore, all right? I mean, why do you think we came up here? The Network doesn't need the two of us for some two-bit little cable hearings. Harris wanted us to be around to help you help your friend. That way he can borrow some of your commitment."

"I thought he just liked to watch me make a fool of myself."

Shirley smiled. She has a pretty smile. "That, too," she said.

I grinned back, and we finished our breakfast.

Our discussion of The Hidden Anguish of Harris Brophy was a lot more enlightening than anything we were able to get out of Roger Sparn. He didn't want to talk in the first place—he seemed to be in hiding. Shirley and I split up to look for him. I finally tracked him down in the lobby men's room. I stood next to him and began to grill him. He conceded everything, then took the position "So what?" Yes, he knew his company had negotiated with Grant Sewall and that those negotiations had fallen through. He himself had met with Mr. Sewall frequently, in Rochester, New York City, and even in Sewanka.

"But I challenge you, Mr. Cobb," he said, as he shot me a pop-eyed glance, "to tell me what possible bearing that can have on the hearings about the Sewanka cable franchise."

Good point, I thought. It sounded even better in his rich, educated voice. Just so it couldn't be said we surrendered without firing a shot, I took a stab at it.

"Well, suppose Mr. Sewall retains an *option* to buy that stock, either under his own name or under the name of some corporation he's formed for the purpose. On his own behalf or as an officer of Whitten Communications. Conflict of interest, wouldn't you say?"

"How so?"

"Well, Whitten Communications has stayed out of the application process expressly because the committee wanted to diversify the number of information sources in this town. Imagine their surprise if they give the franchise to ComCab, and six months or a year later, ComCab is a wholly owned subsidiary of Whitten Communications."

Since he was conceding things, he conceded that, too. "Yes, that would be embarrassing. Fortunately, it's not likely to happen. Good day, Mr. Cobb."

"Yeah," I said. "Good day."

I found Shirley and reported. She was angry at having been cheated out of her rightful share of the work, but she was excited at my theory. "You know, I'll bet that's just what it is! I'm going to get busy on it. Thanks, Matt." She gave me a little kiss on the cheek, which was a bold move for her, and started off. Then she looked back over her shoulder and said, "You're still doing good work for the Network, aren't you? It's like you never quit at all."

If that was supposed to make me feel better, it didn't work. All it did was remind me that with all the running around I'd been doing, I still didn't have one solid thing that could help Dan out of jail.

Shirley's words came back to me: ". . . willing to attempt something important you might fail at." It was funny. I'd never considered my ability to fail one of my good points. I still didn't.

CHAPTER 19

"Would they kill me? They'd kill me and go out for pizza!"
—Jack Klugman, "The Odd Couple" (ABC)

I stood there sighing for a minute or so, then started to walk around. I went out to Whitten College, toured the campus, revived some memories. After a few hours of that, I went back to the inn for lunch. Then I decided that if I wasn't doing anything, I couldn't even fail properly, so I decided to get back in business.

This time I'd work at the problem from the other direction and let Grant stew for a while. The hypothesis was simple—if Debbie had been killed by a karate blow and Dan hadn't done it, who had? Where else could we find a karate expert, preferably one who would be willing to kill an heiress for hire? If we could find him, in this theory, we could learn everything.

It was an intriguing idea. Symmetrical. With Grant, we'd—okay, *I'd*—picked a suspect and worked inward toward the crime. Now, I'd take the crime and work outward.

Okay then, where's the best place to look for a karate expert? In a karate school, of course. The only problem with that was Sewanka didn't *have* a karate school. I'd have to find the nearest one.

Like a good Boy Scout, I used the resources at hand. I was in a town with a great institution of higher learning in it. The greatest thing about it at the moment was the fact that the library was open on Sundays. It was nice to be on campus anyway. Made me feel young. I went out there again.

Land in that part of New York State is plentiful, but a lot of it is vertical or at least on a slope. That's certainly true of the land Whitten College is built on. Over the years, the campus has expanded over the edges of the plateau it originally occupied, around the bottom, and up all the neighboring hills. This has led to two unchangeable facts of life on campus. There is no place to park closer than a quarter-mile away from your destination; and at least half of that quarter-mile will be up or down stairs built into hillsides.

Alumni are notoriously conservative where the alma mater is concerned, and I was grinning despite my shin splints when I reached the top of the flight of one hundred three concrete steps that ran up the side of Heart Attack Hill, at the bottom of which I had parked the Network car. I was glad the young whippersnappers had to go through this ordeal on the way to class in the morning. It would build character.

As I walked across the quad toward the library, it was driven home to me again just how young these whippersnappers *were*. It was discouraging. How had these infants gotten into college, for crying out loud? I'd never been that young, not even in high school. I was beginning to think this trip had been a mistake.

Spot fit right in, though. He'd caught his breath after the great climb, and he was prancing around the cool green grass of the quad, sizing up the other dogs and allowing the coeds to coo over him and stroke his white fur.

After a while, he decided that was too tame, so he leaped into the middle of a Frisbee game, got position on an Irish setter, timed his jump perfectly, and intercepted the disk. He ran over to me with it, with an expression on his face that said, "Look what I found."

The setter had chased him, and the two dogs pretended to fight for a second, then began sniffing each other, which has always struck me as a hell of a way to make friends. I looked up to see a pretty dark-haired girl in a tee shirt and gym shorts looking on the dogs with an indulgent smile.

I held up the Frisbee and said, "Yours?" She nodded and clapped her hands, so I flipped her a soft little forehand throw that she snatched out of the air with a little jump that did great things for the tee shirt.

Then she waved to me and said, "Thank you, sir."

Sir. I felt like running over to her and showing her my driver's license. Hell, I wasn't thirty years old yet. I don't even like it when little kids call me sir.

I knew I wouldn't be long, so I told Spot to wait for me outside the library. The Frank Humphrey Fish Memorial Library was still standing, which was by no means a foregone conclusion. It had been one of the great scandals ten years ago when, with the construction half completed, some unnamed hero at the architecture firm discovered that the original plans had neglected to allow for the weight of the five million or so books this thing was being built to house. They'd had to reinforce floors and walls with cables to make it safe.

Other than that, it was a lovely place. My alumni card got me in, and a quick look at the directory confirmed my memory of where the phone books were. I went to the desk and asked for the Yellow Pages for the area codes 607 (where I was now), 716 (Buffalo), and 315 in case they (whoever "they" was) had gone as far away as Syracuse to get the hypothetical karate killer. Of course, as long as I was being hypothetical about it, there was nothing to say they hadn't flown somebody in from New York or even Yokohama, but I figured I might as well play my highest percentages first.

The nearest place was in Elmira, and there was another in Binghamton, a few in Buffalo, a couple in Syracuse. I'd start phoning them tomorrow.

I gave the phone books back to the attendant, then turned to go. That was when I decided somebody was following me. A middle-aged guy on the tough side of nondescript, whom I'd first spotted puffing along after me up the stairs. We'd even exchanged a few words. I remembered he'd said, "These stairs can kill you." Now he was waiting just outside the phone-book room, reading a magazine. He got up just after I'd walked by.

It could have been a cop, of course. It would be sort of encouraging if it was, in fact—it would mean that Chief Cooper wasn't 100 percent satisfied with the case against Dan, that his men were still looking for evidence. If they were, they might even turn up something that could help.

Of course, if it *wasn't* a cop, that was even more encouraging. It meant I had somebody worried. I had stirred something up. I was overcome with an urge to have a talk with this guy.

I had it all planned by the time I'd pushed my way through the revolving doors and out onto the campus. I wouldn't even make him suspicious; I'd just walk back to my car. At the bottom of the stairs, the path zigzags around the corner of the geology building. All I had to do was duck into a doorway after the first zag, then tap him on the shoulder as he went by.

I told Spot to come along, and took off briskly across the quad. I was going briskly because if you want to pull something like this on a tail, you want to have him moving fast. He has less time to react that way, less time to think.

Of course, it also gives *you* less time to think. I was so busy making a list of questions I wanted to ask this guy, I neglected to ask myself the most important question of all: Why was he following me in the first place?

I didn't think of that question until I already had the answer to it, after my tail had closed the distance between us, then run up to me and given me a stiff push from behind at the top of the stairs.

It was an especially effective move, because I had to turn it into a clumsy dive to avoid landing full on Spot (who was preceding me down the steps) and smashing him into a furry disk. I remember thinking, as I flew head first toward the concrete, that I had wanted to be moving fast down these stairs, but that this was ridiculous. Then I asked and answered the question—he was following me because he wanted to *kill* me. I just had time to curse myself for having made it so easy for him before I hit.

My left knee hit Spot a fairly solid blow in the flank (he'd turned to see what I was yelling about), and he let out a yip that had quite a lot of "What's the big idea?" in it.

Still, he got off lightly. Instinctively, I put my hands out to break my fall. I also nearly broke my wrists. I did flay the palms of both hands, but I had enough brains to let my elbows give with the shock. This resulted in my smacking my forehead on the edge of a step, but it was a lot better than the broken neck or the fractured skull the pusher had planned for me. "These stairs can kill you," I thought grimly.

The way I landed enabled me to turn the momentum of my fall into a sort of sideways roll, which let me absorb most of the impacts on my elbows, knees, and upper back. I could feel a little more skin being scraped away every time I hit.

Spot was yipping as he ran along behind me. He probably thought I was having fun. Some fun. With the pain, and the way the hillside was spinning in my vision, I was beginning to get a good idea of what a piece of glass in a kaleidoscope feels like.

I must have fallen over sixty of those hundred plus steps before I stopped, sprawled drunkenly against a railing. The world kept spinning.

Spot caught up with me, sniffing me for a second to see if this battered wreck in torn clothing was the same guy he'd been with at the top of the stairs, then started to lick the scraped places on my face. Not only did it burn like fire, it started me speculating on the dire results of subcutaneous applications of dog spit on the healing process.

The world stopped spinning, and I pushed Spot away. He took it good-naturedly enough; he was glad to see I was able to move. I sat up, winced, made a cry of pain, then forced myself to look back up the stairs at the place I'd fallen from. There were little double splotches of blood soaking into the concrete, marking every place my hands had touched the stairs. I squinted up into the afternoon sun, trying to see if my pal had hung around to see the results of his handiwork, but I couldn't spot him. He either had a lot of confidence in himself, or he had decided during the early part of my trip that I was going to survive and split so I wouldn't be able to identify him.

I still wasn't sure I was going to survive. I steeled myself, then took a look at the palms of my hands. And immediately wished I hadn't. Blood, and dirt, and torn skin, and little pieces of rock embedded in them. There was one particular pebble stuck in my left palm. I couldn't stand the thought of its staying there. I forced the fingers of my right hand to bend enough to pick it out. The effort left me sweating and short of breath.

Even as I sat there, I could feel my battered muscles beginning to tighten up on me. Rigor mortis of the living. I was hoping somebody would come by and help me down the rest of the way, but no such luck. This was Sunday. Few students would get down past the main quad today.

With a curse and a groan, I fought my way to my feet and made my way to the bottom of the stairs. It took maybe twenty minutes, the worst twenty minutes of my life.

It was slightly less terrible on level ground, and I staggered toward the Network car with one thought on my mind: home. Someplace where I didn't have to move. Someplace where I'd be safe.

There was just one problem: I couldn't open the car door, couldn't close my fingers around the handle. As it was, it was hell trying to get the keys out of my pocket. The only way I could do it was to turn the pocket inside out and get *everything* out, change and all.

Then I stood there, trying to balance the stuff on the small undamaged portion of my hand, until I finally realized that even if I managed to get into the goddam car, there was no way I was going to be able to grab the steering wheel to *drive* it.

I staggered on some more, looking for a telephone. I finally found one, after a painful trek of what seemed like six light years but was probably more like sixty yards. I had dimes among the change that was still sitting on my hand, but I decided to use a quarter—easier to handle.

If that had been a rotary-dial phone, I don't know what I would have done. I had enough trouble pushing the buttons. The pain kept filling up my mind and making me forget how many numbers I had dialed.

Finally, though, I hit enough, and somebody's phone started to ring. I counted along, praying I'd gotten the right number, praying that she was home. Four. Five. I refused to panic. The phone company asks you to let the phone ring ten times, for a full minute. Seven. Eight. Ni—

"Hello?" I allowed myself to breathe when I heard Eve's voice.

"Thank God," I said. It came out more like a croak. "Eve, this is Matt. I need you. Now."

She chuckled low in her throat. "Why, Matt. This is so *sudden.*"

"Not like that, goddammit! I'm beat up and bleeding, and I can't move. Come and get me before he comes back and tries to kill me again."

"Before he *what?*"

"Kills me. Eve, hurry up, all right?"

"You'd better not be joking, Matt. I was in the shower."

"No joke. Eve, I mean it."

"All right, then. Where are you?"

Wonderful. I'd been about to hang up when I heard her say all right. I put the phone back to my ear and gave her directions. Then, as a character building exercise, I tried to stay on my feet until she showed up.

CHAPTER 20

*"Of all the happenings of ee-volution,
Oi reckon this comes closest to a miracle!"*
—David Bellamy, "The Botanic Man"
(Thames TV and CBS Cable)

About two hours later, I met the district attorney, Mr. R. John Wernick, known in newspaper stories and on ballots as Jack. Ever since Jimmy Carter became President, politicians have gone for nicknames in a big way. I expect someday to see an election between somebody named Ace and somebody named Fatso.

Jack Wernick wasn't the type to qualify for either of those appellations. He was the platonic ideal of a politician. He was tall; handsome, but not too handsome; young, with just enough wrinkles to imply wisdom; and well dressed without looking as if he'd spent too much money on his clothes. He had a great smile, and a great voice. Les Tilman had said he was the best criminal lawyer in this part of the state. Everybody said he was ambitious. It took about nine seconds in his presence to see everybody was right.

I didn't dislike him for his ambition. Disliking a man like District Attorney Wernick for his ambition would be like disliking a tiger for his hunger. I disliked him because he was so damned smug he made me want to push him down a flight of stairs. He was going to ride to power on the back of Dan Morris, and he didn't care who knew it.

"Well, of course, Mr. Cobb," he was saying, "all we have is your word that you were attacked. It's a pity your dog can't testify."

Spot snarled at him, a sentiment I heartily approved. We were in Wernick's house, in a book-lined study that would make a perfect setting for a campaign add. Chief Cooper had brought Eve, Spot, and me there after we'd shown up at headquarters to deliver the news. The chief had seemed impressed; at least he'd felt it was important enough to share with the DA.

I'd already been to the emergency room at Sewanka General. My hands had been bandaged like a boxer's, my back painted like a brick wall. I had thick gauze pads taped to my left elbow and both knees, and I had a Band-Aid stuck at a jaunty angle on my forehead.

They'd given me some Darvon tablets for pain, but I hadn't taken them yet; they made me drowsy, and I wanted my wits unimpaired when I spoke to the law.

Fat lot of good it did me.

I held up my bandaged hands. "How'd I get these, then?" I asked. "Reaching into a Cuisinart?"

"Please," he said, holding up a hand of his own. "Don't get me wrong, Mr. Cobb." The expression on his face said that was his cross to bear in this world. People kept getting him wrong. "I'm not saying you didn't take a nasty tumble down those stairs. And, believe me, I sympathize with your injuries—"

"But I'm still a liar, right?" I tried to sit back, decided that was a mistake when seventeen million nerve ends screamed in protest, and went back to the edge of my chair.

"Now, Mr. Cobb," he said sadly. I'd gone ahead and gotten him wrong, anyway. "You've had a very upsetting experience—"

"Lots of them. Including this one."

He ignored me. "—and that experience has come after you've been exhausting yourself in a hopeless cause. It's no wonder you might wish to read something into your accident that would help your friend."

I stood up with a sudden effort. If I'd tried to do it slowly, my body would have rebelled. This way, I tricked it into submission. I groaned, I don't know whether from pain or from frustration.

"Look, Mr. Wernick—"

"No, Mr. Cobb, *you* look." The great smile was gone now. Apparently, he'd given up on my vote. He leaned forward in his chair and placed his hands on the desk. "The penalties for giving false information to the police can be severe. I am giving you your only chance. Ask Ms. Bowen, why don't you? She will tell you that what I've said is true. And she'll also tell you my case against Morris is cast in steel."

Eve spoke for the first time. "The penalties, Mr. Wernick, for a district attorney who fails to do his duty are also severe. As I'm sure I don't have to tell you." Her long red hair danced around her face like flames of anger.

"Mr. Cobb has filed an official complaint," she went on. "Unless and until he decides to withdraw it, you, Chief, are obligated to investigate it, and *you*, Mr. Wernick"—the word "Wernick" sounded like a new species of insect, the way Eve said it—"are obligated to bring charges and prosecute if the chief's investigation so warrants. Shall I cite statutes?"

I like a good, honest fight. I like to see enmity out in the open. Things are much healthier that way. That's why I was delighted to see the look of cold fury on Jack Wernick's face. Battle lines were now firmly drawn, and I had another reason to try to get Dan off. I owed the district attorney a pie in the face.

That, apparently, was a common sentiment. Outside, Chief Cooper came over to us. A frown was folded in among the usual creases.

"I'm sorry, folks. I just wanted you to speak to Wernick so you'd know what you were up against. He's making a crusade out of this case, and he won't take any back talk."

"Has he been getting any?" I said. I was glad now I hadn't taken the Darvon.

"How's that?" the chief said.

"If this is such an open-and-shut case," Eve said, picking up on my thought, "and my client's guilt is so manifest—that's the official position, isn't it?—well, if that's the case, why should Wernick be getting any back talk at all? Who has other ideas? Based on what evidence?"

Cooper grinned at us. "I think I've said all that's wise. You two are sharp, aren't you? But I should tell you this—there's no *serious* opposition to Wernick's ideas; it's just that he won't listen to *any* opposition."

"What about you?" I asked.

"Like Ms. Bowen says, I'm a public servant. I know my duty. You want to come in tomorrow, look at some mug shots, try to find the guy who pushed you?"

"I sure do." We made it for ten o'clock Monday morning. The chief made a note of it, then climbed back in his Land-Rover and drove off.

So did we. Eve was smiling as she drove. I asked her what the hell she was so happy about.

"Like old times, wasn't it?"

"Wasn't what?"

"Our talk with the chief. You spotted the key phrase—"

"Right. Then you hammered him with the heavy artillery. Ouch." I shifted on my seat. "How much pain do you have to be in before you can die?"

"Don't be a baby," Eve said. I told her I was being brave,

that if I gave in to my impulses, I'd be a whimpering blob of protoplasm.

"Well, you'll take your medicine, and that will help. We'll stop at my place first."

"What do you mean, 'first'?"

She smiled again. "Resolved," she said, "that Matt Cobb, having made of himself a helpless cripple, will need, at least tonight, a personal servant to feed him, walk his dog, change his bandages. You take the negative."

"No, thank you. About taking the negative, I mean. You're an angel, Eve. I was wondering how I was going to open the can to feed Spot. But answer one question for me."

"Yes?"

"Does this go on the bill?"

"Oooh, Matt. I'll get you for that."

"I surrender."

"Too late. That was a tasteless remark."

"That's half my charm, my tastelessness. Wait till I'm better, at least, before you exact your revenge, okay?"

She said we'd see about that. She parked outside her house, and left Spot and me in the car while she threw some things in an overnight bag.

Eve started cooking while I went to take a shower. In its way, the shower was worse than the fall itself, because the shower was my own idea. The water burned like acid, and the soap was 99$\frac{44}{100}$% pure torture. Still, it felt good to get rid of the sweat and grime that had accumulated during the day; the folks at the hospital had cleaned only the wounded areas.

I got out of the shower, then dried off by patting myself with the towel, the way you dry a baby. Then I shrugged into briefs and a pair of cutoffs.

Eve saw me emerge, went in, and turned the water off, then sat me on a kitchen stool and repainted and rebandaged me.

"You do nice work," I told her. "You could have been a doctor instead of a lawyer."

"Simple first aid," she said. "I picked this all up in the Camp Fire Girls."

"WoHeLo means Love," I said, and she laughed.

I got on an old, loose sweatshirt and sat down to supper. Eve had made chicken soup, a wise idea, since I could handle a tablespoon fairly well. It was good stuff, and I told her so.

She blushed prettily and thanked me.

I looked at her closely, trying to figure out what was going on here. After all, it hadn't been too long ago that she'd told me she hated me, this tough, competent courtroom fighter who was defending a man she thought was guilty because that was what she did.

Now here she was, all motherly and domestic. She even tucked me in when the pills took effect, and I went to bed.

I got about six hours of deep, dreamless sleep, and I felt much closer to human when I woke up later Sunday evening. I joined Eve and Spot in the living room, where the radio was playing softly. It was the local soft rock station, the very one I used to listen to when I lived in Sewanka.

"Hello, Matt," Eve said. "I've been making friends with Spot. He's a lovely dog. So intelligent." She was also still being domestic. On her lap was a needlepoint pattern, a unicorn in a field of flowers.

I yawned and sat carefully in Dan's best chair. "Intelligent enough to be wonderful to people who feed him anyway." She told me I was terrible, and I agreed. "Did you walk him?"

"Yes, we had a nice walk." She made a few stitches, humming along with the radio. After a while, she said, "Matt?"

I'd closed my eyes. They popped open, though I didn't feel startled. "What is it, Eve?"

"What do you think is the reason you were attacked today?"

"I wish I knew. They've got Dan stuffed and sewn and ready for the oven, as far as I can tell. Why take a chance that someone will believe me and start to doubt Dan's guilt? Unless, of course, they've got Wernick pegged pretty accurately. Which, come to think of it, doesn't seem too difficult."

"No, you're right about that. Of course, another aspect of it could be that they didn't expect you to survive the fall."

That made me sort of laugh. "Once I started falling, I didn't expect to survive either. If basketball hadn't gotten me used to falling on hard surfaces, I'd probably be in a refrigerator right now."

Eve held her needle in midair, looked at her work, bit her lip. Then she put her hands together in her lap and looked at me sadly. "Matt," she said, "I'm going to ask you a question. I don't want you to get mad, and you don't have to answer. Even if you do, I promise this will be the end of it, and I'll never mention it again."

I smiled at her. "All right, Counselor. Go ahead."

She took a breath. "All right, then. Have you considered the possible effect on yourself if you find out Dan really is guilty?"

I had promised not to get mad, so I didn't. I just said, "Ah."

"You have an enormous emotional investment in his innocence," she went on. "It's almost as though you were out to prove your *own* innocence."

I closed my eyes again. My battered body seemed to throb the more I thought about an answer. Finally, I said, "You're right, Eve. If it turns out Dan killed Debbie, I'm finished."

She shook her head angrily. "You can't do that! That's my whole point. You can't let your own self-respect depend on the actions of someone else. I'd be a basket case if I let that happen!"

"We've had this argument already," I told her. "Look. The guy is the best friend I have ever had, and I'm not a lawyer. The only reason I'm here is that I believe in him. He has looked me in the eye and told me he never killed her. For me, that's that. It *has* to be, don't you see that? Or what kind of friend am I?

"That's the key thing. Not whether he killed Debbie. Hell, if Dan did it, that would be a classic crime of passion —anybody can lose his head and lash out."

"Not you," she said. "You're too strong."

Now I shook my head in sadness. "Don't bet on it, Eve. I know what I'm capable of. Someday, somebody's going to say the wrong thing at the right moment, and I'm going to kill him. I've been afraid of that happening since I was twelve."

She told me I didn't mean that, and I let it go. I got back to the point. "Anyway, if Dan did do it, which I still don't believe, that means he's used our friendship to back up a lie. If I can't trust him, I can't trust anybody. I think that answers your question."

She smiled. "Not really. The question was, 'What would you do if?'"

"Oh. I don't know. I don't really want to think about it."

Eve said nothing. She went back to her needlepoint. Spot was amusing himself by rolling around on on Dan's mat. I closed my eyes again and listened to the radio.

The DJ played Bob Dylan's "Just Like Tom Thumb's Blues" by request. I wondered idly what kind of masochist would request that number—it's a work of genius, all right, but it's one of the most surrealistically depressing works in history.

I listened to it, losing myself in the song; when Dylan got to the last line, in which the singer decides to go back to

New York City because he believes he's "had enough," I started to shake.

Not tremble, *shake*. As if I were hooked up to one of those exercise machines. As though I were being electrocuted. Nothing like that had ever happened to me before, and I started to panic, which made it all the worse.

Spot saw what was going on and started to whimper. Eve looked up at the noise and saw me. She was alarmed.

"Matt! What's wrong?"

"I—I—I—" I was trying to say, "I don't know," but I couldn't do it. Eve said, "You'd better lie down," and practically carried me back to the bedroom and put me on the bed.

"Are you cold? Do you want a blanket?"

I shook my head no, and she lay down beside me and held me tight and spoke softly to me. "It's all right, Matt, don't worry, I'm here, everything's okay, it's all right—"

Eventually, it worked. I stopped shaking and lay on my back, breathing hard. "Jesus," I said. "There goes my macho reputation."

Eve started to laugh. "You idiot." She shook a finger at me. "You've been worried sick about your friend for days, you've quit your job, there's been an attempt on your life, you're a physical wreck, and you've taken powerful medicine. I think your macho reputation can survive a case of the shakes."

"You sure you're not just saying that to make me feel better?"

"Positive. This is what I do to make you feel better." She leaned over and kissed me.

It was soft and warm and welcome, and when she stopped, I put my bandaged hand behind her head and pushed her back to me with my wrist.

"Goodness," she said at last. "This takes me back to the waterfall days."

"You remember." I grinned.

"Mmm-hmm. I've got it filed under unfinished business. You walked out on me before we could finish it." Very gently, she touched my cheek. It was all I could do to keep from shaking again.

"Yeah," I said. "Really makes me wish I weren't a physical wreck."

She kissed me again. "Nonsense," she said. "This is how I've always wanted you. Helpless." She bit my nose.

"But I'm all bandaged up—"

"I'm into gauze." Her hands were soothing and exciting at the same time, and her lips were magic.

I still wasn't totally convinced. "How the hell am I supposed to make love to you? I can't use my hands. I can't use my elbows."

She was naked now, pink skin and red hair making a beautiful pattern of flesh and flame. And the freckles. Millions of them. She was working on getting rid of my clothes, gently sliding them past the sore spots.

"Well?" I demanded.

"Shut up and stop worrying," she said. "We'll think of something."

And, by God, we did. Lots of things. Much later, when it was over, we slept holding each other, and I felt warm and safe. And loved.

CHAPTER 21

"Snatch the pebble from my hand."
—Keye Luke, "Kung Fu" (ABC)

Eve appointed herself my official chauffeur beginning Monday morning and wouldn't take no for an answer.

"What about your other clients?" I asked.

"Matt, I'm capable of worrying about my own business, really. Not everyone's like you, you know, ready to immolate himself at the drop of a hat. Believe me, if I couldn't afford to take the time to do this, I wouldn't. Besides, somebody has to keep an eye on you."

"Oh," I said. "Well, since you put it that way, the first stop is police headquarters."

Chief Cooper was waiting for us with a three-foot-high stack of mug shots. Eve took one look at the pile and decided to go to her office after all. I would call her when I was ready to go somewhere.

The chief watched her go. "Nice woman," he said.

"I like her."

"I could tell. How is this all going to affect your friend's defense?"

"How do you mean?"

"You got Eve Bowen convinced he's innocent?"

"I don't know. I've got *me* convinced he's innocent. The only other people I really have to convince is a jury."

"Yeah, twelve people who'd rather be somewhere else." He started to dig through the books. "Look, Cobb, I don't know what it is about you, but you've got me thinking, too." He pulled out one of the fat volumes and thumped it down on the table in front of me.

"Here, look at this one first."

"Oh? You have a candidate?"

He looked at me grimly. This whole episode was against his better judgment, or maybe just against his sense of the fitness of things. It wasn't right for a cop (at least it wasn't right for Merce Cooper) to be helping someone work against a good solid arrest.

"Just look at the pictures," he said. "Call me if the guy who pushed you down the stairs is in there."

I looked at the book. I had a certain amount of difficulty with it at first, because my hands still hurt too much for me to turn the pages. I was damned if I was going to ask for a policeman to come sit at my elbow and flip pages for me, so I struggled along until I hit on the wet-thumb method. If I wet the side of my thumb and pushed hard, I could slide the paper in toward the spine until there was a nice bend in the paper I could get my left hand under. After that, things went much more smoothly. We cripples develop ways of dealing with things.

With the physical technique taken care of, I got involved in looking at the faces. Before long, I realized it was only the format of the photographs, the full-face and profile, with numbers underneath, that made these men seem like criminals. They were just faces, handsome, ugly, and in between, looking into the camera with varying degrees of interest. It could have been the portfolio of the Upstate New York Toyota Dealers' Association, or a college alumni bulletin, or any other seemingly random collection of male human beings.

I guess the moral of all that was that you can't tell a criminal until he pushes you down a flight of stairs.

As I sat there, awkwardly flipping the pages, I began to wonder what the hell I would do if this guy turned up again. If I punched him, I would score an instant knockout—of myself. I'd probably pass out from pain if I just made a fist. I could get a gun, but unless I could figure out a way to pull the trigger with my thumb, that wouldn't do me a whole lot of good either.

And what if some karate expert came after me? After all, I thought, that karate-type bruise didn't just grow wild across Debbie's throat. Somebody put it there, somebody, I told myself, whose existence I as yet had no way to prove. Just possibly there was a karate killer for hire at large somewhere. Possibly. Who might be after me next.

That was a frightening thought. Even if I were in top condition, that would be enough to scare me considerably. As it was ("... how I've always wanted you," Eve had said. "Helpless."), I dealt with it the only way I could—I refused to let myself think about it.

Patiently, methodically (well, not really, but that's how it would have looked to an outsider), I made my way through that book of mug shots. Rarely have I done anything more boring. They were all beginning to look alike. It must have been something like this, I decided, that had led Professor Lombroso to his theory of "the criminal type."

Then I found him. Third from the right, second row from the bottom of a left-hand page. I blinked hard, then took another look. It was my pal, all right, no question about it.

"Are you sure?" Chief Cooper demanded when I called him over.

"Positive."

"Crap," he said. I asked him to elaborate.

"This is the guy I thought it might be," he told me. "You're absolutely sure? Okay. His name is Fred Stampe; he works out of Rochester. He's about your age, maybe two or three years older."

I looked at the picture again. "Come on, he's got to be fifty. Look at that face."

"I know, I know. When I was with the State Police, we had to go through stuff like that every time we busted him. He was this big student activist, you know? Tried every drug from alcohol to Xylocaine, and was working on y and z when he got into the strong-arm racket. Of course, the way he burned himself up free-basing four, five years ago, like that comedian, you know—"

I told him I knew.

"Like him. One of the first cases of that I ever came across. That didn't do his looks any good, either. Between dissipation and scars, he looks twenty years older than he really is."

"Jesus," I said. "How'd you know it was him?"

"I still don't know it was *anybody*, Cobb. Not officially. The DA had better not hear about this until I'm ready for that to happen. Is that clear?"

"Sure. But what made you think of him in the first place?"

"It's his style, pushing you down a flight of stairs like that. Along with the description you gave me, of course, but it's more the MO. This guy is a total acorn shell."

"A what?"

"A nut case."

"I thought you had no sense of humor."

He smiled at me. "This is a pose to make the witness feel comfortable, all right?"

"Oh. Yes, it's working very well. I'm quite comfortable. Do go on."

"Thank you. Anyway, after Stampe burned himself up,

he sort of went off the rails completely. Stopped taking drugs and opened this storefront drug-free place. One of those do-it-yourself encounter things, you know? And he gets pretty good results, too."

I said that all sounded very commendable.

"Oh, sure. Only trouble is, Cobb, this guy commits murders for hire to finance the goddam place! The only reason he's loose is that we've never been able to pin anything on him."

"You said something before about his style."

"Yeah. Ever since he stopped pouring chemicals into his body, he's become all-natural. Never uses knives, guns, ropes, poisons, anything like that. He kills on the spur of the moment, using whatever's handy."

"Like a flight of stairs," I suggested.

"Exactly. You ran into him in the library. Another time, he did one of his numbers just outside a library in Utica. Beat this guy's head in with a portfolio of bird paintings. The victim had just checked it out. Like I said, whatever's available."

"Cute."

"I'll tell the world it's cute. It's what helps keep him out of the clink, too. There's never a weapon to trace to him, and when we do manage to get a witness, he makes a big noise about how we're picking on him, because we always harass reformed drug users, especially the ones who are trying to help people. Another thing about him, he makes it a point to meet the people he's supposed to kill, exchange a few words with them. He gets away with it, too."

"He spoke to me on the stairs," I said. "The question is, is he going to get away with killing Debbie Whitten?"

"He didn't do that," the chief said flatly. "That's really not his style. He doesn't know karate, and he never deals with anybody, man or woman, indoors. That's another one of his hangups."

"If he's not involved in Debbie's death, what the hell did he try to kill me for?"

"I don't know, Cobb. I'll have the guy picked up, if I can. You be careful in the meantime."

I called Eve, then picked up a paper to read while I waited for her to come and get me. It was more of the same. This time they'd asked some psychiatrists why Dan wouldn't be able to get off, even with an insanity plea.

I mentioned it to Eve as she drove us toward Route 17.

"I know," she said, "I read it this morning. I think Mr. Whitten is really being foolish about this. He wants Dan convicted without delay, but every time he prints something like this, he gives me another excuse to get a change of venue on this case. And more *cause* to get one. Any judge would have to concede that it's impossible for Dan to get a fair trial in this town."

"Even the ones the old man got elected? The ones who owe him?"

Eve completed the interchange, merging with the eastbound lane with caution and prudence before she answered. "Even those. If they let the trial take place here, a guilty verdict is almost certain to be overturned on appeal, especially if I'm denied a change of venue in the first place. No judge likes to be reversed, especially on something like that."

I had mixed emotions about it. It was nice to think that Dan would be able to go somewhere and get a fair trial, but we were talking about the prospect of months, or even years, with no guarantee of a favorable outcome. I hated to be crass, but Dan and I put together didn't have the money to finance something like that.

Then I got to thinking about Mr. Whitten. "I think he wants to believe he's doing it himself," I said.

"What's that?" Eve had been watching the traffic.

"The old man. It was his daughter who's been murdered. He wants Dan's head on a sharp pole, but he's too civilized just to lop it off. So he's going to do it symbolically, going to destroy Dan in the minds of all the people who've ever liked or respected him. And a lot who haven't even heard of him."

Eve nodded and said that made sense to her. "But there's one thing I wanted to tell you. Okay, the trial is supposed to start Thursday. But the first thing I'm going to do is ask for a change of venue. If I get it, there'll be a delay of at least three weeks while they find someplace else to hold the trial —I'm going to ask for Plattsburgh or Massena, as close to Canada and as far away from Whitten's media influence as I can get.

"If I *don't* get the change, I'm going to make this the most tedious, nit-picking, contentious jury-selection process in the history of New York State jurisprudence. Every time I see a juror I don't like the looks of, I'm going to challenge for cause and make Wernick fight it out. I'm going to hoard pre-emptories like diamonds, and I'm going to get every instance of a venireman's being exposed to Whitten-controlled media propaganda into the record. Every single one. It'll take at *least* three weeks."

I wanted to kiss her. "That's the spirit," I said. "I'd applaud if I could."

"I'll take the wish for the deed. Anyway, Matt, I wanted you to know that you're not on any tight last-minute deadline."

"Unfortunately, I am."

She shook her head; her red hair bounced prettily. "Matt, I just explained to you—"

"That's not it. There's an old political proverb that applies here, too: 'If you throw enough mud, some is bound to stick.' That's the whole idea behind the change of venue, isn't it? The concept of it? If people are told enough times someone is guilty, read it in the newspaper, hear it on TV and radio, they believe it, no matter what evidence comes out in court. I don't want my friend to go around for the rest of his life known as the one who killed that girl and got away with it. Every day I fail to clear him brings that closer to happening."

Eve kept her eyes on the road. "You know, Matt, you aren't God. You shouldn't try to be."

I had a flash of anger. I turned on her, about to ask her if she expected me to be content with things the way they were. Then I decided to hell with it, she was probably right.

Time for a little levity. "Why not? My mother always wanted me to be ambitious." It wasn't a great line, but it worked.

When we finished laughing, I said, "Eve, you know you saved my life last night, don't you?"

"Don't be stupid. I wanted you."

"I needed you. I didn't even know it. Thank you for knowing it."

"Anytime," she said. She showed me a small smile. "Tell me again why we're going to Elmira."

"We are going to Elmira because this karate stuff has been driving me nuts. I'm going to talk to the guy who runs the karate school where Dan goes to keep sharp."

"In Elmira?"

"It's the nearest one to Sewanka. Besides, I hear it's quite good. The guy who runs it just happens to like it there."

"Well, it'll be a new experience for me, at least. I've never visited a hojo before."

I started to laugh. "What's so funny?" Eve demanded.

"A *dojo*. A karate school is a *dojo*. A 'HoJo' is a restaurant with an orange roof."

"One letter off, big deal."

"It is a big deal. Look at the difference between 'acme' and 'acne.'"

She conceded the point. We listened to the radio and discussed trivia for the rest of the trip. I suspect she led the conversation in that direction to keep me from brooding, which was damned nice of her, only it didn't work. When I want to brood, nobody can stop me.

There's an old joke that goes, "My hometown is so small, the Mafia is Swedish." Well, there are a lot of towns in New York State smaller than Elmira, but nonetheless, the Elmira Karate School was owned and operated by Stan Lundqvist. The martial arts, I learned rooming with Dan, are remarkably free of prejudice as to what kind of person should be teaching them. Stan was a former national champion, and his belt was black enough to please anybody.

Except for his outfit, he was the stereotypical Swede, big, rugged, blond and blue-eyed, with a square chin and a loud laugh. When he found out I couldn't shake his hand, he bowed, and it seemed so natural, I bowed back. He shook Eve's hand and told her how beautiful she was, the way somebody else would comment on the weather, that is, as if it were a self-evident fact.

Lundqvist saw my bandages and immediately jumped to a conclusion. "If you want to sign up for lessons, mister, don't do it in anger, or because you want to get back at somebody. Go home, wait until you're all better, and decide with a quiet heart that you want to study karate." He pronounced it the Japanese way, *kah-rah-tay,* equal stress on all three syllables.

I reflected that if I waited until my heart was quiet, I'd be too old to move, let alone learn anything. "No," I said, "it's not that." I introduced Eve and myself, and told him I'd like to talk to him for a little while. He said that was fine with him, as long as we didn't mind tagging along while he watched his class.

We marched into the main room. On a wall-to-wall mat, sixteen housewives were bouncing around sixteen other housewives. When Lundqvist told them to, they went at it the other way round. I couldn't help noticing that every exercise ended with the tosser poised to finish off the tossee with a shot to the throat.

Without looking at us, Lundqvist began to speak about Dan. "I used to warn him about his temper, you know. He has a very bad temper."

"I know that," I said. "I used to share an apartment with him. He told me he took up martial arts to control it."

Lundqvist nodded. "That's a very important part of the discipline. Dan was very devoted—he was a better pure stylist than I am, to tell you the truth—and I thought he had his anger licked. Apparently not."

"I don't think he killed that girl."

Lundqvist turned to look at us for the first time. His eyes were very blue, very cold. "That doesn't really matter, unless the newspaper accounts are wrong when they say the police placed him on the scene of the crime by proving he smashed part of a stair railing."

"No, that much is true."

"Well, then. He lost his temper and destroyed something in anger. Once he'd gone that far, I'm surprised he only hit the girl once."

"If he did it," Eve added. I looked at her in surprise—that was my line.

"If he did it," Lundqvist echoed. "I have mixed feelings about that. It doesn't seem possible anyone else could have, does it?"

"Not at the moment," I said.

"And yet, knowing Dan's style as I do, I'm surprised he would use *shuto*—"

"What's that?" Eve asked.

"A blow with the side of the hand," I said. I'd picked up *something* living with a karate expert for four years. "The kind that killed Debbie."

"Exactly right," Lundqvist said. "I was surprised he used that blow instead of *gyaku zuki*, which is a direct strike with the knuckles, like so." Without a pause, the karate expert dropped into a crouch, extended his left arm, then pulled it in, at the same time extending his right. The whole thing took maybe an eighth of a second, and I could almost hear the air move aside with the force of the blow.

I just hoped I'd never be on the receiving end of one of those things. I asked Lundqvist if he had ever heard of a martial arts person who would mess people up for hire.

"You mean like a *ninja?*"

"I guess so. Yeah. The *ninja* came into being to do things the samurai were too honorable to do themselves, right?"

"That's right. But why do you ask? Have *you* heard of something like that?"

I had to admit I hadn't.

"I didn't think so. Not in this country, at least. Don't let the martial arts movies fool you. This is too difficult a discipline for the sort of person who thinks an easy way to make a living is to beat people up."

That made sense to me. Why study for five years to learn a way to terrorize innocent people when you could get a gun and do it in five minutes? If terrorizing people is what you want to do, I mean.

I had mixed emotions about this news. On the one hand, it soothed my fears concerning my theoretical Mad Karate Killer. On the other hand, it shot down one of the few theories that would have cleared Dan.

Lundqvist asked if there was anything else he could do for us. Eve asked if a person who had no skill in martial arts could just happen to hit a person the right way by luck. Lundqvist's answer was a flat no. That seemed to cover it, so we thanked him and left.

Eve drove us back to Sewanka. She dropped me off at Dan's place. "Can you work the keys?" she asked. I reminded her I'd locked up behind us this morning.

"Besides," I told her, "I'll have Spot do it if I can't."

Spot gave me a dirty look. Eve said, "Okay, Matt. I'm going to the office. I'll be back here around six." I said that was fine, but it was way better than fine.

"Did we learn anything in Elmira?" she asked.

"Not unless you did," I said.

"I learned what *shuto* and *gyaku zuki* are."

"See? Nothing is ever wasted, is it?"

"No, of course not." She put her arms around me and kissed me. "Be careful, Matt," she whispered. "Somebody is beginning to like you a lot."

Then we kissed again. She got in the car and drove off.

CHAPTER 22

*"...So here he is, America's Top Trader,
TV's Big Dealer..."*
—Jay Stewart, "Let's Make a Deal" (ABC)

I got the door open with a modicum of trouble and a tolerable amount of pain. As soon as I'd unlatched it, Spot pushed his way in, scooted into the kitchen, and sat looking up at the cupboard with his tongue hanging out.

"All right, all right, I get the message," I said. Lucky for him, Eve had thought to buy him a *box* of dog food instead of the canned stuff he usually got. This way, I could take the box in both hands and pour. He would have starved otherwise.

For an aristocrat, Spot eats like a slob. He sucks it in like it's the only meal he's ever had or is ever likely to get, and he makes little pig grunts the whole time.

I loved him anyway. Still, it usually is a lot better for my own appetite if I don't watch him eat. This time, though, I watched him because he bothered me. He'd been bothering me ever since I'd had that dream. There was something I ought to be remembering, something right in front of my face ...

I thought I had it for a split second, and maybe I did. Unfortunately, I couldn't remember what the damned thing was when the split second was over. That kind of thing drives me nuts, because the more I think about it, the farther away it gets. But I can't stop thinking about it.

Spot didn't care, the insensitive wretch. He just cleaned out the bowl, then looked up at me with big cow eyes in a shameless attempt to get seconds.

You have to be firm with him at times like that. "No," I said. "Too much ash in this stuff. It's bad for you."

Spot didn't care about ash content, but he caught on he wasn't going to get any more. He shrugged, as if to say it was worth a try, then ran off to the living room to play on the mat.

And I stood there like a dope trying to remember what it was I wanted to remember. I shook my head. Rick and Jane Sloan had spent thousands of dollars for attack training and obedience training for that pooch. Why couldn't they have invested a few more bucks and taught him how to talk?

I was saved from this, and from thoughts even more foolish, by the telephone. It's not difficult to pick up a receiver with both hands, but it does take a certain amount of concentration, and that cleared my head very nicely.

"Cobb?" I admitted it. That established, the voice went on to demand, "Where have you been all day?"

"Poisoning squirrels in Whitten Park. Who is this, Grant?"

"Yes. I want you to—"

I make it a rule never to let myself be bossed around by my adversaries. Unless they have a gun pointed at me or something.

"I want *you* to be a little polite," I told him. "Start by explaining why it's any of your goddam business where I've been."

"It doesn't matter. I'm calling from Mr. Whitten's office. He'd like to talk to you."

"What about?"

Grant sighed deeply. Mr. Patience. "I don't know, Cobb. I would guess that it concerns the murder. Will you come here, now?"

"Right now?"

"That's right."

This news brought with it a whole new set of foolish thoughts. What does the old man want with me? There was, of course, only one way to find out.

"All right," I said. "I'll be there shortly, since you've asked me so nicely. Good-bye."

I called a cab and crossed to the south side of town, where the headquarters of Whitten Communications stood next to an enormous shopping mall. More accurately, it was part of the mall. Back in the mid-sixties, when he decided to put his TV, radio, and newspaper operations under one roof, A. Lawrence Whitten had had the clever idea of letting some of his land pay for the rest of it. The mall and his headquarters building went up at the same time.

They looked the same, too. Both were huge rectangles of pinkish concrete, with bits of mica mixed in for shine. The afternoon sun was glinting off them now, making the whole place look like a temple of truth.

I went in and told the receptionist who I was, and that Mr. Whitten was expecting me. She pressed a few buttons and confirmed it, then gave me a clipboard and a pen, and told me to sign in.

I grabbed the pen with my thumb and proceeded to produce a specimen of my signature that Spot could have written. It seemed to satisfy the receptionist, though, and soon I was being led through the building by a long-haired intern from the college.

I was a little surprised at the big man's office. The Network had led me to believe that everyone above a certain level in the communications industry—above *my* level, I hasten to add—gets to have as an office his favorite room from the palace at Versailles.

Mr. Whitten had the fishbowl, or one of them—that glassed-in kind of office that most modern city rooms have. This particular city room had about seven of them; executives had the workers surrounded. Either Mr. Whitten liked to keep an eye on *all* his people, executives included, or he had been a big fan of "Lou Grant."

Needless to say, Mr. Whitten had the biggest fishbowl with the cleanest glass. That's all the sign on the door said, by the way: "Mr. Whitten." If you didn't know who he was, you had no business in the building.

The kid opened the door for me (which was nice of him) and scurried away, as though he were awed to be in the company of Greatness. I stepped inside and greeted the great.

Grant looked at me and said, "Cobb." I told him his name was Sewall, and Mr. Whitten his name was Mr. Whitten. This little bird-behavior bit of territorial display taken care of, I was invited to sit down.

The old man looked as if something sour had grafted itself permanently to his tongue. He worked his tongue around his mouth as though trying to dislodge it. Finally he said, "Cobb, what the hell do you think you're doing?"

"Listening to someone who, I was told, wanted to talk to me. Waiting," I added, "for him to say something."

"Be your age, Cobb," Grant said. For the first time since I'd known him, Grant didn't look as if he'd been molded from plastic. He had some lovely purplish circles under his eyes, and he seemed to be squinting against the harsh fluorescent light.

"My age," I said, "is increasing all the time, and nothing is happening. What do you want?"

The old man's voice got tight, and I had a glimmer of

how he'd managed to triple the family fortune at a time newspapers all over the country were going out of business.

"No, goddammit, Cobb, we're here to talk about what *you* want. Why are you hanging around Sparta?"

"I like the local newspapers." This was amazing. "Also, I'm going to be a witness at a trial. If it goes that far."

"What do you mean by that?" he demanded.

"It means I'm going to prove he's innocent, that's what it means." Grant looked disgusted, and Mr. Whitten was turning red. They both had things they wanted to say, but I got there first.

"But forget about that for a minute. Are you sitting there with the thought in your mind that you're going to run me out of town? How do you plan to do it, short of mob violence? You print things; did you ever hear of a document called the Constitution of the United States?"

That really upset Mr. Whitten. Patriotism was *his*. How dare I refer to the Constitution in an argument against him?

He snarled at me. "Listen, you little *guttersnipe*—"

That made my day. I had never heard anyone (except me) spontaneously utter the word "guttersnipe."

"—and listen well. I can arrange things so that you—"

"Mr. Whitten!" Grant cut in sharply before his employer could say anything that could be used against him later. Mr. Whitten shut up, and took a few moments to get control of himself.

I spent the time thinking. "I could arrange things so that you—" the old man had said. So that I *what?* Fall nose first down down a flight of concrete steps?

I already had the Organic Hit Man after me (I was sure of it, even if Chief Cooper wasn't), and he had to have been hired by *somebody*. On the other hand, it's kind of silly to issue a threat about something that's already been tried. If that was the threat Mr. Whitten was about to utter. I mean, he could have been about to say, "I can arrange it so that you never get a copy of one of my newspapers that doesn't make your fingers black and disgusting from cheap ink." Or something equally innocuous.

Damn Grant, anyhow, for interrupting him. I began to wish I had Brenda with me; she had the knack for handling him, if that episode at the cemetery had been any indication.

Mr. Whitten was calmer now. He opened his mouth again, but this time he gave out the sweet sounds of reason.

"Now, listen, Cobb. Your devotion to your friend is understandable, even admirable. But you must ask yourself if he *deserves* this devotion."

"Go on," I said.

"He doesn't, you know," Grant put in. "You've made all sorts of sacrifices for him. I understand you even quit your job."

"It wasn't that great a job," I said.

"And for what?" Mr. Whitten was carrying the ball again. "For a young man who spends years developing his body into a deadly weapon, then, in a fit of anger, unleashes all that power against *my daughter!*"

There was a lot of anguish in those last two words. Mr. Whitten hid his face in his hands.

My turn now. "Mr. Whitten, your grief is understandable and, though you might not believe it, to a certain extent I share it. I want to see the murderer punished. I want to see *all* murderers punished. I just don't think Dan is the murderer."

He looked up from his hands with tears in his eyes. *"You know he is!"*

I was suddenly very aware of being in the fishbowl. In spite of everything, I was embarrassed for the old man. I looked around. There were no noses pressed against the windows, but that didn't mean the reporters didn't have some idea of what was going on. Nobody goes into journalism if he doesn't have an extra measure of curiosity.

"This is pointless," I said. "We're all getting upset arguing questions that will be decided in court." I got up to leave.

"Wait a minute," Mr. Whitten said. "Sit down, Cobb." I sat. The old man was disgusted, whether at himself, or me, or both of us, I couldn't say.

"You'll never prove him innocent," he said.

"I think I will."

"You'll just stir things up. Confuse things. You can't prove he's innocent, because he's not, but—"

I interrupted again. The sympathy I had felt for a moment was rapidly disappearing. "Nobody has to prove he's innocent. The district attorney has to prove he's guilty."

He nodded grimly. "I know. That's why, with your running around and confusing everything, you might create a loophole to let that murderer go free."

"And?"

"I want you to stop. I want to know what it will take to make you stop."

So that was it. Any sympathy that was left died in that instant, replaced by a cold contempt.

"I see. Well, I'll just bet you've got a few ideas already, haven't you?"

Grant took over. Grant was very suave. "Well, Matt, seeing as how you're out of a job currently, and knowing how Whitten Communications is always looking for good people—"

It was the first time in my life he had ever called me Matt. I didn't like it much. "I could come to work for Whitten Communications?"

"I think that could be arranged, Matt," Grant said.

"Of course, we wouldn't want to make this public too soon," I said.

"No, that wouldn't be . . . tactful."

No, I thought, you bet your patrician ass it wouldn't be

tactful. We'd be in front of a grand jury so fast your fillings would melt.

"You could," Grant oozed, "take a vacation first." The old man nodded, eyeing me warily as he did so.

"I always wanted to visit Australia," I said wistfully.

"I hear it's a wonderful place."

"Only thing is, it's very expensive to go to Australia."

"That could be . . . ah . . . taken care of."

"Oh," I said. "How nice. Shall we talk about exactly *how* it can be taken care of?"

Grant's mouth dropped open. This was too raw, even for him. First you announce you're corrupt. Then *later* you talk over dollars and cents. That apparently was the way it was done in his set.

"Right now?" he asked.

I grinned amiably at him. "Sure, no time like the present. Hold on just a second, though, all right?" I stood up again. "Grant, would you mind opening the door for me?" I held up my hands.

Grant was too stunned to ask what I was up to. He opened the door without a word.

I stood in the doorway and yelled to the city room at large. *"Hey! Everybody!"* Heads popped up from behind word-processing terminals. "May I have your attention please? Can you all come down to Mr. Whitten's office? Your boss is about to offer me a big bribe to go away and let my best friend rot in jail, and I want witnesses!"

It got a big laugh from the crowd, which was gratifying. Even more gratifying was the yelp of anguish it got from the two in the office.

"Get out of here!" the old man said. He was practically screaming.

"I'm going, all right. I'm going to take a shower, and burn these clothes. You make me very sick."

I walked out and strode through the city room. There

were smiles on several faces. Apparently Les Tilman wasn't the only journalist left in Mr. Whitten's employ.

That was a loud crash behind me. I jumped, then spun to see what the hell was going on. I was just in time to see the splinters of one of the glass walls of Mr. Whitten's office falling from the frame. The old man had thrown a bottle of ink at me, through the glass. His aim was good, but his throwing arm was a little weak. The ink bottle was spinning at my feet.

I picked it up in my clumsy, two-handed way, and walked back toward the broken window. Glass crunched under my feet, and it occurred to me that I didn't want to fall down on this stuff. Still, I was committed to the gesture. I've always believed God watches out for romantics.

I stood in front of the jagged hole in the window, cradling the ink bottle in my hands.

"You know, old man," I said, "you spoke before of a man who spent years turning himself into a deadly weapon. Well, under the right circumstance, *anybody* can become a deadly weapon. You can, for example, use a newspaper to destroy people, people who haven't been convicted of *anything* yet. What kind of consideration does someone like that deserve?"

I looked at him for a moment, holding his eyes and making sure he got my point. Then I said, "I think you dropped this." I lifted my arms and softly tossed the ink bottle on the desk.

God *does* watch out for romantics. As the bottle hit the desk, the stopper came out of it, and Grant and A. Lawrence Whitten both got splashed with ink. Very symbolic. And it served them right.

CHAPTER 23

"*Here are some more tempting ideas you might try.*"
—Ed Herlihy, "Perry Como Presents
    the Kraft Music Hall" (NBC)

Shirley Arnstein was waiting for me outside.

"Is this a coincidence? Are you going my way? Answer the second question first."

She laughed. "Yes, I have a car in the parking lot. No, it's not a coincidence. There's something I wanted to tell you about, and I couldn't find you. I just went down the list of people who might know you until I got to Les Tilman, and he told me you were here."

Typical Arnstein efficiency. Les Tilman was undoubtedly the best source in town, so naturally Shirley had latched on to him during the two days she'd been in Sewanka.

"He said you were talking to the Big Boss. Anything interesting happen in there?"

I shook my head. "A crashing bore," I told her. "That's a joke which I will explain later, if you're interested. What's your news?"

Shirley's eyes were bright. "You'll never guess," she said. If she has a fault, that's it. She hoards her discoveries the way a kid hoards cookies.

"NBC has gone out of business," I suggested as Shirley led the way across the blacktop.

"No, but ComCab has," she said over her shoulder.

I stopped in my tracks. *"What?"* I demanded. I'm renowned for my ability to ask shrewd and penetrating questions.

"Well, not *completely* out of business. But they're not hanging around for the end of the cable franchise competition here."

"Are you sure?" Stupid question. Shirley was always sure.

"Mmm-hmm. I went looking for Sparn—I still haven't been able to talk to him face to face, you know—and at the hotel, they told me he'd checked out. I dug up one of the committeemen, and sure enough, Sparn's told them he had to leave town. He hoped it wouldn't affect ComCab's application, but it would have to, wouldn't it, Matt?"

It was practically unheard of, pulling out at this late date. It costs a lot of money to apply for a cable TV franchise, even if you do it honestly. But practically all of that money is spent up front. ComCab's big investment, legal or otherwise, had already been made. Why pull out now? It was like throwing all that money away. The representatives were there to answer questions from interested members of the public. The committee would look very bad if they were to award the franchise to someone who wasn't there.

When we reached the car, I said, "Did Sparn give anybody a reason for leaving?"

"Sort of. He told the committeemen he was needed back in Rochester to confer on a presentation in a major city."

"I bet the good representatives of Sewanka loved that. Does anybody believe him?"

"For the record, they do. Of course, if any of the committeemen have been receiving gifts from Sparn, they'll suspect something is fishy."

That made me smile. "Boy, they sure will. I wonder how

many of them will be honest men and stay bought and vote to give ComCab the franchise anyway."

"Harris is coming back tonight. Do you want to talk to him tomorrow morning? He told me he thinks he's found out something important."

"To the Network," I said.

"Of course, Matt. Harris thought you'd be interested to hear it, though, anyway."

"Sure," I said. "What the hell. Give me a call when you're ready, or better yet, come on over here. The fewer knobs I have to turn, the sooner these damn hands will heal."

Shirley said that sounded fine to her. She dropped me off at Dan's apartment, I turned one more knob, went inside, threw myself across the bed, and tried to take a nap.

I got one, if you call five minutes a nap.

The phone rang. I swore at it, but I answered it. I always answer the phone. It was Chief Cooper.

"I understand you paid a little visit to the local newspaper today, Cobb," he said.

I rubbed my eyes without thinking. It turned out to be a good idea—nothing has ever made me wake up faster than the scraping of adhesive tape over my eyelids.

"I was invited," I said.

"Raised quite a ruckus, didn't you?"

"I did not. I was insulted and offered a bribe. The bribe was even more insulting than the insults. All I did was yell a little."

"You didn't spill ink on old Mr. Whitten and his assistant?"

"Do they say I did?"

"They sure do. Mr. Whitten called me personally, a few minutes ago." That figured. Grant would have had too much sense.

"Well, then I must have done it," I said. "Actually, it's a

game the old man invented called KoKo the Klown roulette. He throws an inkwell at me, then I throw it back. We do this until it comes open and one of us gets covered with ink."

"I told you, Cobb, I hate jokes."

"Me, too, goddammit!" I listened to that going across the wire, and I was astonished to discover I really meant it. "I'm tired of that senile old jerk trying to get me to dance for him because he has money, and because he thinks my friend killed his daughter."

I took a breath and calmed down. "Listen, Chief, here's what you do. You go investigate this whole incident. Question everybody who saw what was going on. Unless he's managed to terrorize his whole staff into lying for him, you won't be arresting anybody unless I press charges. Against him. Have we got a deal?"

"All right, Cobb," he said. "Just cool down. I just want to make sure you keep your nose clean."

"Sure. Right to the point of holding the Kleenex for me."

"Don't be disgusting."

I told him I'd try, and he grumbled a little, then hung up. The chief was beginning to remind me of Lieutenant Cornelius U. Martin, Jr. of the NYPD, who has known me all my life, and who functions as a combination friend/conscience/mother hen/nemesis whenever our paths happen to cross. I wondered if all cops were like that, or if it was something I brought out in them.

I didn't wonder about it too long, though. I went back to sleep.

I woke up to find myself looking into Eve Bowen's dark blue eyes. That is a wonderful way to wake up. "Hello," I said.

"Hello, Sleeping Beauty," she said. "Do you always sleep this much?"

"Only when I can." I started to rub my eyes, but this time I caught myself. "What time is it?"

"Six o'clock. I'm a punctual person. You really are, you know."

"I really are what?"

"Beautiful when you sleep. You look like a little boy. You even hold your arms as if you had a Teddy Bear in them."

"I forgot to bring my bear. That's why I had to cultivate you this trip."

She smiled and looked happy and kissed me. "Anytime, Matt."

I felt good. That worried me. I said, "Eve, I have been treated rotten by many women in the past."

She was changing out of her work clothes. No hurry, no blatant seductiveness. Just natural and beautiful.

"I've been stepped on by men a few times, too," she said. "So what?"

"If you're going to break my heart, do it *now*, okay? Before I start to depend on you too much."

She did exactly the right thing. She came over to me and ruffled my hair and said, "Idiot."

I put my arms around her. "Sit down and tell me about your day."

"Routine," she said, with the shrug of a freckled shoulder.

"Well, wait until you hear about *my* day." I told her, in detail.

"This is getting crazy, Matt," she said when I had finished.

"*Getting* crazy?"

"I don't know what any of it means."

"I don't either. How many freckles do you have?"

She laughed. "What does *that* mean?"

"Serious scientific inquiry. How many?"

"I don't know, thousands."

"Well, you're going to find out. I'm going to kiss every last one of them. Take the rest of that stuff off."

"Oh, Matt—"

"Come on, woman! I may be a helpless invalid, but my brain still cries out for knowledge."

She kept laughing, but she complied. She had lots of freckles. After a while, she wasn't laughing. We didn't have dinner until a long time later.

CHAPTER 24

"You don't have to ask for it—he knows what you want."
—Catherine Deneuve, Chanel No. 5 commercial

Dan's mail came early the next morning. There was the usual stuff—some bills, some junk mail, nothing personal. One envelope was from the Whitten College Alumni Association. It said Dan could spend a great vacation at a low price because of the Association's group rates. Computers are great ironists sometimes. A human envelope addresser would have known that Dan was likely to spend his vacation this year in scenic Attica.

A little later, Brenda Whitten showed up. I was watching "Agony of Love," the Network's longest-running soap opera, and thinking that it had happened at last—that my life had finally become as confusing and foolish as the script of the show.

A car horn went off, and Brenda called my name from the parking lot outside. I lowered the volume, then went to see what she wanted.

She wanted in. She was standing at the bottom of the stairs, with one hand holding her crutches and the other on the railing.

"Hello," I said.

"Hello. Will you help me up the stairs, or do I have to use these stupid things?" She raised the crutches.

I went down the stairs, lent her a shoulder, and helped her inside. Spot was delighted to see her. He jumped up on her and practically knocked us both over.

I got her seated. Spot settled down next to her chair and closed his eyes contentedly. I said, "Well, Junebug, what brings you around here today? Besides an automobile, I mean." The way she smiled told me she'd been about to make the same joke herself. "Which reminds me—I didn't know you could drive."

"Oh, sure," she said. "For ages. I just sit a little over to the right and use my good leg on the pedals. Passed my driver's test first time. Proud of me?"

"Inordinately," I said. "You could have taken the time to get dressed, though." She was wearing cutoffs, sneakers, and a tee shirt.

"I dress like this all the time," she protested. "This is what I was wearing that day you drove up to the house, when Dan was pitching batting practice for me."

"You were wearing a bra then."

"Don't be a fuddy-duddy," she told me. "And don't be a hypocrite, either." She held up a filmy something Eve had left behind the chair. "Unless," she said, "your taste in underwear is a little strange."

"That's different. I've had designs on her virtue since college, whereas you've always been like a sister to me."

Brenda got serious; she was no longer bantering. "Don't worry about my virtue, Matt, all right? I'm the only one who has to be worrying about my virtue."

"All right," I said. "No offense meant. Can I get you something to drink?"

"Orange juice?" Brenda said.

"Lots of that. Think I'll have some myself."

I went to the kitchen and poured. Clumsily, but I didn't

spill much. I gave Brenda her glass; she took a sip, then licked her lip with a pink tongue. She made it a very provacative gesture. Sirens and alarms went off in my head— what the hell was this silly kid up to?

Brenda said, "Is she pretty?"

"Is who pretty?"

She smiled at me. It's irritating to be patronized by a teenager. "The woman who leaves things like this in your living room." She held the garment up again.

"This is Dan's living room," I said.

"True," she said. She took another sip of juice. "But this being here isn't from anybody of Dan's. The only woman he had over here was Debbie. And Debbie could wear only pure cotton stuff. She had some sort of crazy skin condition. Did you know about that?"

"I found out recently." I think I said that. I wasn't paying a whole lot of attention. I got one of my horrible feelings that something important had just happened, and I'd missed it. I looked at Spot. I looked at Brenda. I looked at the TV set, where silent figures were walking around doing things that made no sense at all.

I snapped out of it. Brenda had been talking. "I'm sorry." I said. "What were you saying?"

"I was asking you again if she's pretty."

"Oh. Yes. Yes, she is."

"Prettier than me?"

"Prettier than *I*," I said. Brenda was certainly endeavoring to look pretty right now. She was working body language for all it was worth. The curve of her neck was an invitation, the shape of her mouth practically an order. I decided that objectively speaking, the answer to Brenda's question was no. Eve was not prettier than she was. Not that it made any difference.

"Come on, Brenda," I said. "You didn't come here to play 'Who's the Fairest of Them All' with me, did you?"

She sighed, "No, I guess not. I heard about your run-in with my father yesterday." Then she gave a little giggle. "You ruined his favorite tie."

"And?"

"And I guess I came to apologize."

"Don't mention it. It's nice of you, but unnecessary. You're not responsible for your father's actions."

"In a good family, people are always supposed to feel responsible for each other. Or so I've heard."

She looked down at her lap for a second, then back at me, clear-eyed and defiant. "I hate him, you know. I hate all of them. Father, and Grant, and all the reporters, and the servants, and people on the street. And Debbie for... provoking her own mur-murder"—Brenda was beginning to cry now—"and Dan for not getting away from her long ago, and I hate *you* for stirring things up! And I hate myself. More than anybody."

Anything else she was going to say dissolved into sobs. I handed her a Kleenex and tried to make her feel better. I told her everyone feels like that sometimes, usually with a lot less reason.

She did not stop crying; I don't know if I had anything to do with it.

"I'm sorry you hurt your hands, Matt," she said at last.

"Me, too," I said. "Hurts like crazy, and I've got to learn all sorts of uncomfortable ways to do things."

"I know," she said. It was almost a whisper.

The fittings on her false leg gleamed at me like an evil grin. Well, Cobb, I thought, you certainly have put your foot in it this time. I started to apologize, but Brenda cut me off.

"It's all right, Matt. Nice in a way. We can be cripples together."

"I said I was sorry."

"I'm not mad. I mean it. We could be close together."

"Knock it off, will you?"

She struggled to her feet and walked toward me. "Don't let the leg bother you, it's just one less thing to get in the way. Some guys get turned on by it—".

"Stop it." I didn't know what else to say. I was sad and sorry for this lonely little rich girl.

"You're the big one for being there when your friends need you, aren't you? I thought *I* was your friend. I need you now."

"Not that way," I told her. "You're punishing yourself. And you're testing me. But it won't work, the test won't. You think you'll find out if I'm turned off by you because you're a cripple—your word. If I like you, I ought to be willing to take you over on that mat and screw you. But then how do you know I'm not just feeling sorry for you? Or one of the guys who get turned on?"

Brenda was looking at the floor.

"How often do you run this little experiment?" I asked.

She mumbled something.

"What?" I demanded.

"I said, 'Why should you care?' "

I took her by the shoulders. "Goddammit, Brenda, have a little *respect* for yourself. You've got every conceivable thing in the world going for you except *one stupid leg!* If you give yourself half a break, you can turn out to be one hell of a woman."

That really started the waterworks. She fell into my arms, held me tight, like a little kid, and irrigated my shoulder for a good five minutes. Then she looked me in the face, still crying, said, "Oh, Matt," picked up her crutches, and left.

CHAPTER 25

"News, of the hour, on the hour."
—ABC radio

"I don't have any proof," Harris Brophy said about an hour and a half later, "but then, I've got a corrupt mind. I don't *need* proof."

Harris was kneeling on Dan's karate mat, arranging and rearranging a collection of Xerox copies. The documents represented all sorts of things: mortgages, promissory notes, leases, personal services contracts, even a birth certificate. It was an amazing collection for a few days' work. None of it, as Harris had said, was proof, but taken all together, it was suggestive.

"Isn't this terrific?" Harris said. He was practically glowing with enthusiasm. Harris enjoys finding evidence of corruption the way a kid likes opening presents on Christmas morning.

"It's interesting, all right," I said. "It would be quite a coincidence if they borrowed all this money from mob fronts by accident."

Harris grinned up at me. "Now, Matt, don't be hasty. I didn't say these were all mob guys. I said my sources in three different federal attorney's offices *think* they're mob guys."

I grunted. "Close enough. I've got a corrupt mind, too. What are you going to do about this?"

Harris shrugged, then got up and took a chair. He scratched his head. "I guess I'll have to turn it over to the FCC and let them worry about it. I don't like the idea; I think it would be more fun to run this down myself. Still, we don't want the Network in trouble. The only thing I have to decide is which office to bring it to. Canandaigua is closer, but New York has all the people we're used to dealing with."

"Go to New York," I said.

"Why, Matt. I know that look on your face. You've come up with something."

I didn't know I had until he'd mentioned it. "Yes," I said. "I want you to—" It occurred to me I had no right to want him to do anything. "You might want to ask Marty Adelman a question. Show him a picture, maybe." I told Harris what I had in mind in greater detail, and as I did, he grinned wider and wider.

"It adds up," he said. He nodded slowly, doing the arithmetic over. "It adds up, none left over. Of course, this is just tidying up as far as the Network is concerned."

"Not at all," I told him. "If you put ComCab out of business, they lose all the franchises in the cities they've already won. New people will have to take over—a new chance for Network Cable in every city."

Harris bit his lip. "Of course. I bow to the wisdom of the master."

"Oh, shut up," I told him. "Hurry back to New York and find out what Marty says, will you?"

"Sure, Matt. But you realize, don't you, that even if you turn out to be right about this, that it won't be one bit of help toward getting your friend loose? It'll be a setback, if anything."

"I know. That's why the sooner I know, the better." I put through a call to Les Tilman at the newspaper, and arranged for Harris to come by and pick up the photo we wanted. Les laughed and said I should come pick it up myself, such interesting things happened when I was around. I was not amused.

As soon as I hung up, the phone rang. It was Eve.

"Matt," she said. "I just got a phone call from someone who says he knows something about the case, something that could clear Dan. He wants to talk to us."

"Where? What did he have to say?"

"He wouldn't talk on the phone. He says he's close to the Whittens, though, and he can definitely help. We're to meet him by the drumlin out on the county road in forty-five minutes. Do you know the place I'm talking about?"

"Sure. Look, Harris Brophy is here. I'll have him drop me off at your office. We'll save time that way."

She told me she'd be waiting. After I put the receiver down in my clumsy, two-handed way, Harris said, "Anything?"

"Who knows? Probably a crackpot out to send a lawyer and her helper for a ride in the country." I called Spot, who perked up his ears and grinned and came immediately to heel. He'd probably thought he was going to be left behind, so this was a pleasant surprise for him.

It wasn't an altogether selfless move on my part. I had, after all, been pushed down a flight of stairs. I wasn't nattering with fear or anything. I just wanted Spot around, just in case. Because there was a chance, just a chance, that this might be something. Possibly a trap, but I didn't care. Dead center was the worst trap of all, and it was high damned time I got off it.

Harris offered to come along. He hates being left out of anything, but I told him no thanks. The trip to New York was top priority for him.

"I suppose so," he said. "I'll pick up that picture, say good-bye to my shy sweetie, then head for New York. I think I'll let Shirley stay up here for a few more days and keep an eye on you."

I told him that if he expected me to resent that, he was wrong. "Don't joke about her, Harris," I told him. "Shirley is a great kid, and she loves you like crazy."

"I know it," Harris said, but there was no conceit about it. He seemed genuinely distressed. "I'm nowhere near good enough for her. I don't know what to do about it. I like her, too. I'd rather not hurt her, but—"

"Listen, Harris. I've got a wild suggestion, here, but it's crazy enough to work."

"I'm listening," he said.

"Try real hard and *make* yourself good enough."

He took his eyes off the road to look at me for a second, then worked his jaw as if tasting the suggestion. "Hmm. I never thought of that. I'll think it over."

And on that optimistic note, we arrived at Eve's building. Harris said he'd try to get to Marty Adelman and call me tonight. I thanked him and went inside.

CHAPTER 26

"Don't make me angry . . . You wouldn't like *me when I'm angry."*
—Bill Bixby, "The Incredible Hulk" (CBS)

I had high hopes for that little jaunt into the country but low expectations. It is an acknowledged fact that most crimes in this country are solved when someone calls the police, or (more frequently), the police call somebody, and the somebody tells them who did it. It could be just that simple now, but I didn't believe it. This had to be a crank, just another nuisance in a long series.

It was a nice drive, though. The leaves had come out in brighter shades of green during the past week. Spot and Eve seemed to be having a great time, but I was still thinking of what it would mean if what I suggested to Harris turned out to be true. I wasn't enjoying *breathing*, let alone watching the scenery.

We drove north on the old county road, past Hans's restaurant and damn near out of Sewanka jurisdiction altogether. I was starting to get edgy; Eve noticed and said, "It's not much farther."

"Good," I said. "What are we supposed to do?"

She didn't even remind me of how many times she had already told me. High-quality woman, I thought. Then my brain chose that moment to remind me that the last woman I'd thought of that way had made me a fool, and very nearly a corpse. I set my jaw, told my mind to shut up, and listened to the lady lawyer.

". . . Thirteen miles past the interchange, there's a rest area where you can stop the car and sit at a picnic table a little way into the woods. We're just supposed to sit at the table and wait for him, if he's not there first."

"Did he say how long we're supposed to wait?"

"No," Eve said. Then she shrugged. "We'll give him a half hour or so, then take off. How does that sound?"

"Fine, fine." I chewed the tips of my fingers. I usually chew a knuckle at a time like that, but I couldn't get at them. I was getting that uncomfortable, unstable feeling that happens when my brain is about to present me with something, welcome or otherwise. It feels like my blood is carbonated and my skull is filling with fizz.

"There it is," Eve said. She pulled off the road into a little paved-over part of the shoulder. Someone had made a flagstone path into the leafy glade, and when I got out of the car and stood up, I could see the picnic table in the middle. No one was there yet. A very restful scene.

"This stinks," I said. "Wait here with Spot, Eve." Just because *I* was willing to walk into what could turn out to be a trap, that didn't mean I was planning to bring Eve with me. I figured she'd do as I asked and let me handle things. Silly me.

"Matt, I'm not a child. Besides, he said he wanted to talk to *both* of us. If he sees only me at the car, or only you at the table, he might just turn around and go, and we'll never learn what he has to say."

She had a point. I thought of another one. If she waited at

the car, our putative trapper would be able to drive up, do something terrible, if that was what he had in mind, and drive off. And I wouldn't be able to do a damned thing about it. "Okay," I said, "let's go. But let's keep about twelve feet between us."

"Why?" Eve wanted to know.

"Humor me, all right?" I figured that this way, one of us and the dog would be available to come to the other's assistance if someone jumped out from behind a tree and grabbed us. Eve walked on the path; I kept off it to the right. I let Spot make his own way through the woods; he could get back soon enough. He took off, chasing a butterfly.

I should give up figuring.

The attack came from behind a tree, all right, but no one grabbed anything. I felt something oily and wet splash against my leg at the same time I heard Eve yelp, then start to sputter.

I turned around to see Eve with her hands at her mouth. There were large dark stains on her smart suit. My old pal from the library, Fred Stampe, held her by the collar at arm's length. And in his other hand, he held a cigarette lighter.

An empty tin can lay at his feet. "Lighter fluid," he said. "I had a quart can in the car, so I figured I might as well find a way to use it. I want to give up smoking anyway. Bad for you. Clever, huh?"

The Organic Hit Man. Used whatever came to hand.

"Brilliant," I said. Looking at him, I still couldn't believe he was about my age. Nothing about him looked young, except his eyes. They were bright, the eyes of a man who loved his work and was doing a good job. Fred Stampe was flying, on a high more potent that any drug.

"What do you want?" My voice was very cold. I deserved to die for being so stupid, but what had I done to Eve?

"You," he said. "What do you think? You made me look bad, Cobb. I don't like that."

He tugged callously at Eve's collar. "Your boy friend here is something special, Mrs. Bowen. Not one man in fifty would have survived that fall down the stairs. But I don't think you'd survive the burning you're about to get if he doesn't do what I say. Believe me, it hurts. I know." I remembered his free-basing accident.

"*Ms.* Bowen," Eve corrected. Hell of a time for that, I thought.

Expertly, he opened the lighter and flicked the wheel. It lit right off—a tribute to that company's truthful advertising. He started to bring the flame near the soaked part of her sleeve.

"Stop it," I said. "What do you want me to do?"

He took the lighter away, held it at arm's length. "That's better. Walk back to the car—Hey, your hands are bleeding."

I looked at my bandages. Sure enough, they were getting soaked through with red. I had broken open my palms by clenching my fists at my helplessness, forgetting the pain in fury and frustration.

I dropped my hands. Let them bleed. It wouldn't last long. He was going to burn us to death inside the car, or something equally charming. He wasn't going to leave witnesses.

The sunlight filtered through the leaves, bathing everything in a soft green light and giving the proceedings a sort of submarine feeling of unreality. I tried to break it by concentrating on the red of the blood on my hands. On the yellow of the lighter flame.

On the whiteness of Spot's fur.

The Samoyed had given up on the butterfly, and was coming back to join Eve and me. His paws were silent on the new grass of the clearing. I just prayed he wouldn't bark.

At the right distance, I raised my hands again, the signal for Spot to stop.

Then I went insane. It was a cold madness, a fury and a desire to punish that took me over completely.

"Look," I said. "Let her go, and get out of here, and I'll forget about this."

He smiled at me. Good. "Who's making offers? Look, Cobb, I'm sorry I got Mrs. Bowen—excuse me, *Ms.* Bowen—involved in this, but it was the only way to get to you. I have a job to do, you know."

I looked dead at him. "You don't want to screw around with me, Stampe," I told him.

The smile flickered for a second. He was surprised that I knew his name. Then he said, "Such language! And in the presence of a lady, too. How crude can you get?"

"We're about to find out," I said, "aren't we?"

Spot was sitting quietly on the grass, head cocked, ears pricked, trying to figure out what the hell was going on.

"All right, I've wasted enough time warning you," Stampe said.

He started to bring the lighter toward Eve's lighter-fluid-soaked sleeve. Her eyes got round. She'd been silent, but now she said, "Matt—"

And I said, "Hit him, Spot." Three one-syllable words, quietly spoken. That was the kill command.

The result was amazing. Spot's happy face became the face of a wolf, and a hungry one. He rose to his feet, took two quick strides, and sprang at Stampe from behind, knocking him forward on the ground.

I ran forward and grabbed Eve with my bloody hands and pulled her away. Her legs started to wobble, and she sank down against a tree trunk. The lighter fell to the ground and went out.

Spot went for Stampe's throat, and got it. Or at least part of it. Then I saw what was happening, and I realized what I'd done.

"*Spot, out!*" I said, and the Samoyed backed away. Well

trained, indeed. Stampe was bleeding from the base of his throat, but he was alive. I ran over and looked at the damage. Spot had taken hold of Stampe's throat but had obeyed the order to stop before he tore it out.

I leaned a forearm across Stampe's throat, to keep him from messing around once he got over his shock, then looked at the sun's rays filtering through the trees, and thanked God.

I looked around—Spot deserved some thanks, too. Hell, I would have thanked the butterfly that had led him into such a strategic position, if I could find it.

But Spot was still on the job, making sure that Eve was all right. She was just trying to sit up. Apparently, the idea of being made a real Camp Fire Girl had taken some of the starch out of her. Spot didn't want her to get up before he could do his bit, so he started to lick her face.

He gave her a good swipe with that hot, wet bologna slice he used for a tongue. Eve giggled, a good sign. Spot made a terrified noise, and ran away from her with chagrin in his eyes and his tongue hanging out of his mouth.

"What's wrong?" Eve said. She was probably talking to Spot, but he was too busy eating grass to clean his mouth out to answer.

"Lighter fluid," I told her. "You must have touched your face with fluid on your hands. If he hadn't been in such a hurry, he would have smelled it on you and stayed away. It'll be a long time before he licks your face again."

"Is he going to be all right?" Eve was concerned. "He saved our lives, didn't he?"

I nodded. "Not the first time he's saved mine." I took a look at Spot. He was lying in the grass with his tongue still out. He looked hurt and suspicious, but otherwise he seemed okay. I'd take him to a vet as soon as I could, to make certain, but I was already sure about one thing. Spot was a lot safer swallowing a little light fluid than he would have been if he'd killed Stampe. Even with a smart lawyer like E.R. Bowen, a pet who kills somebody has a tough time of it.

I'd kill Stampe myself, if I had to. He started to wiggle a little. I leaned some weight on the arm across his neck and said, "Don't." He subsided. I asked Eve how she was, then told her to come over and tie him up.

She didn't follow orders as quickly as Spot did, but she didn't dally. She got to her feet and joined us. From the expression on her face, I thought she was going to kick Stampe a few times, but she thought better of it.

"Use his belt to tie his feet. Once you do that, we'll roll him over." She tied him with little science but great enthusiasm. As she was finishing his hands (we used my tie for that), she said, "Poor Spot. I hope he's not mad at me."

"He'll get over it if he is," I said. "I'll wait here with Stampe. You drive back to Hans's and call the cops. Chief Cooper, if possible."

"Will you be all right?" She looked at our prisoner. Stampe had been silent since Spot had dropped on him. Maybe he was figuring the angles.

I gave him another one to think about. "Don't worry. If he gets cute, I'll have Spot eat him."

Spot was up and walking around again, and seemed fine. He got curious and came over to join the party. I told him to watch Stampe, and he good-naturedly sat down to do it. Stampe would now move at his own peril.

I watched Eve hurry off to get help and marveled at the beautiful economy of motion. Motion, I reminded myself, that would have stopped forever if it hadn't been for Spot.

"Listen, Cobb. What's it worth to you to let me go?"

"You must be desperate. What are you going to do, write me a check?"

"I'll get the money."

I laughed at him. "I'm supposed to take an IOU, right?"

Wheedling hadn't worked, so Stampe tried threats. "I'm not going to be in prison long, you know. If at all. What can you get me for? Assault? Attempted murder, at the worst? I'll be out in seven years, tops."

"Then what?" I was shooting the breeze with him because I had nothing better to do with my mouth. My brain was bubbling like a witch's kettle. I was afraid of the evil brew it might churn out.

"I'll find you. I'll kill you. It's not hard. I can make it look like an accident. Like suicide. I can make it look like anything. There are weapons all around. I'll find you some night—"

I didn't hear the rest. I froze at a sudden thought that had jumped from the cauldron, vile and dangerous. And so damnably *right*.

It fit. It all fit.

Then Stampe said, "What's the matter? Cat got your tongue?"

And that reminded me of Spot. He had his tongue back in his mouth now, and the happy Samoyed grin was back on his face. I remembered the dream I'd had, where he'd demanded to know why I wasn't listening to him. I hadn't listened because I hadn't wanted to. Spot had solved the case, and all he'd done was follow me around and lick people's faces.

Stampe wanted to know what I was smiling about.

"You were working for Sparn, weren't you?"

"Sparn who?"

"I told you before, Stampe. *I am not to be trifled with.* I want a name, or your head is going to know what a soccer ball feels like."

I think I meant it. If I was right about what I had just thought of, I'd spent a week making a total fool of myself. I wanted to take it out on somebody, and Spot had suffered enough. My best suffering was still ahead of me.

Stampe must have read me pretty well. "Yeah, it was Sparn, all right." Then I asked him why, and he told me. It was just what I figured.

That about settled things. A low whine announced the arrival of the chief's all-terrain vehicle. He came toward us with gun drawn and handcuffs ready.

He smiled at me. "You're full of surprises, aren't you, Cobb? I'm camped not three quarters of a mile from here. Your lawyer friend should be along any minute. They patched her through to me on my radio."

He started for the prisoner. Spot growled at him. I'd forgotten the watch command was still in effect.

I said, "Okay, Spot," and the dog subsided.

The chief said, "Fred Stampe, as I live by bread. I owe you a favor, Cobb."

Stampe spat. The chief turned him over, cuffed him, returned my tie, and led him off to the car. I followed. The chief invited me along, but I told him I'd wait for Eve.

"I mean that about the favor, you know, Cobb." I told him I appreciated it. "Okay, then," he said. "You and Ms. Bowen meet me at headquarters as soon as you get fixed up."

I said we would, and he drove off.

I stood there by the side of the road. I looked back into the glen at the light and the leaves.

It occurred to me that maybe I had thanked God a little too soon.

CHAPTER 27

... "Let's recap and see where we stand."
—Art Fleming, "Jeopardy" (NBC)

"You tell a weird story, Cobb," Chief Cooper said.

"Yeah," I said. "Imagine what I could do if I could just make them up instead of having to act them out."

We were in the chief's office at headquarters. I had nice new bandages on my hands that almost let me forget the mess underneath them. A veterinarian had pronounced Spot none the worse for his taste of hydrocarbon, and everything was swell. Unless the chief didn't believe my story.

"Haven't you talked to Stampe?" I asked.

"Oh, sure. He backs you up. I buy it, Cobb, don't worry about that. It's just an odd one. Sparn hiring Stampe to kill you. Want to know how much your life is worth?"

Eve was at my side. She'd gone home to change, and had come back in her famous jeans and sweatshirt outfit. She had a scarf around her hair. She looked delicious. I could feel a shudder run through her when the chief asked the question.

"Tell me later," I said.

"Sure." The chief smiled. "But let me tell you something. You ever want anyone dead, kill him yourself. Somebody selfish enough to kill for a living is not all of a sudden going to get noble and keep your name out of it once we drop on him."

"Stampe also did the hit-and-run on the Network man in New York, didn't he?" Eve asked.

Chief Cooper nodded. "Just like Cobb here figured, Ms. Bowen."

"I didn't figure it, I guessed."

"Well, just like he guessed, then. Roger Sparn and Grant Sewall hadn't given up on Sewall's coming in to run Com-Cab. This time, though, they were working behind the backs of Sparn's associates, some pretty rough guys. If they found out Sparn was trying to cross them before he was ready for them to find out, it would have been Sparn who was dodging the hit men."

I went to a vending machine and bought a cup of soapy-tasting chicken soup while the chief filled Eve in. I could have figured it out, maybe, if I'd been thinking. Grant knew me, knew I wasn't in town just to hear a bunch of local politicians ask questions. And since he was working with Sparn, he knew the Network was working to shut the two of them down.

They moved fast. Grant called Sparn, Sparn called Stampe, Stampe caught a plane to New York (maximum travel time, including getting to and from airports, two hours), and ran Marty over. Fortunately—or unfortunately, depending on your point of view—he failed to kill him.

They wanted Marty out of the way for a simple reason— Marty had seen Sparn and Grant together in New York. They used to meet there, far away from the home base of either. Marty didn't know Grant, but they feared Marty might de- scribe him to me, and I'd make things difficult.

As I did anyway, once Harris found out about the deal that fell through, the one that precipitated Grant's broken engagement with Debbie. I went around asking questions. On Sunday morning, I'd asked Sparn about it. He called

Stampe, who'd returned to Rochester, a short drive away. I even went back to the hotel, to make myself easy to find. And an hour later, I was flying in for a landing on a slanted runway.

If you ask me, they weren't thinking too clearly—or Sparn wasn't. According to Stampe (and according to Sparn, too, who was in custody in Rochester), Grant had nothing to do with either of the attacks. Of course, Sparn was also saying *he* had nothing to do with the attacks, so we were taking him with salt. But Stampe, who had no reason to be concerned with anybody's welfare but his own, told how Sparn had instructed him that Grant Sewall must never find out about this under any circumstances.

I could see where that made sense. Grant, it seemed to me, was quite capable of blackmailing his prospective partner into a smaller share of the profits once the deal went through. Sparn seemed to have summed him up the same way.

So Sparn panicked. For one thing, he forgot all about Marty, who was still alive and liable to remember any minute. That's what Harris was doing, back in New York, showing Marty Grant's picture. For another thing, he forgot that I wasn't concentrating on him anymore. I had a whole new set of problems to worry about.

The set I still had. I took a sip of my soup and wished for a sudden attack of amnesia. I'd been working like crazy to learn the answers, and now that I knew them, I regretted it. What a mess.

The chief had finished his recital, and Eve was nodding sagely.

"It will be tough to make a case against Grant, the way things are now," she said.

The chief stretched his left cheek, smoothing out the wrinkles. It was a weird effect. "I know, dammit," he said. "Hell, if he's not in on the murder conspiracy, he probably

didn't do anything illegal at all. It's not against the law to try to take over a company. Not even a crooked one. He could say he wanted to clean it up."

I took another oily mouthful of soup.

"Only thing is," Cooper went on, "as far as I can see, this doesn't do a bit of good for your friend. I still like him for the other murder."

Eve was going to argue with him. She opened her mouth, then looked at her old debating partner to make sure we were ready.

She saw me looking into the cup, watching noodles chase parsley flakes. I decided that was as good a metaphor for life as I had ever seen. And it all gets eaten in the end.

She closed her mouth again. The chief shrugged and said, "Sorry. That's just the way it looks to me."

"Yeah," I said again. "Look, Chief, I'm about ready to collect on that favor you owe me."

He smiled. "Good," he said. "Hate to have obligations hanging over my head. What can I do for you?"

"Well, I assume you're going to question Grant about what we've learned this afternoon..."

"Yup. Going to visit him right now, in fact. Unless I decide to have him hauled in. Why?"

"I want you to be finished with him around eight o'clock or so. Then I want you to bring him to the Whitten mansion."

"Easy enough," the chief said. "What is it now, five-thirty? I ought to be able to think of enough questions to last from when I catch up with him until eight o'clock. But why, Cobb?"

"Because I'm going to be there at eight o'clock. I'm going to say some things I only want to say once. Okay?"

Eve wanted to know what I was talking about. I touched a bandaged hand to her cheek.

Cooper said, "Sure, I guess. As long as you don't do anything illegal."

"Promise."

"All right then. But you're not exactly welcome out there. Are you sure they're going to let you in?"

"I'll get in."

It was agreed, then. Eve and I left the building.

"When are we leaving for the Whitten place?" she asked.

"You're not going. I'll get Shirley Arnstein to drive me over."

"I have a right to be there. I'm Dan's lawyer."

"That's exactly why you can't be there."

"Why? What are you going to do, for God's sake?"

I looked into her eyes and saw trust, love, and concern. I didn't want to tell her, but she deserved to know.

"Well, for openers," I said, "I'm going to apologize."

CHAPTER 28

"Thus conscience doth make cowards of us all."
—Derek Jacobi, *Hamlet* (PBS)

I told Shirley to time our arrival for about quarter after eight. I figured it would ease our entry if Chief Cooper were there already, getting the old man curious. I didn't mind if he got him irritated, either. I didn't care about much except getting the whole thing over with.

It had been a long couple of hours since Eve and I had left police headquarters. I told her what I was going to do, and she got angry. She said it was her duty to stop me, but she didn't mean it. Or, rather, she meant it, but she wasn't going to take any action on it. That was very nice of her, I thought. Still, I left her home and took a cab to Dan's place.

I arranged things with Shirley, took a phone call from Harris, telling me that Marty Adelman had recognized Grant's photograph as someone he'd seen talking to Roger Sparn, and, at the last minute, called Les Tilman and told him he might find it interesting to be at the Whitten house this evening.

That was it until Shirley came by. I found out an interesting thing—when you are looking ahead to what you already know will be the worst night of your life, time goes very slowly.

My plan worked. The guard (he was new since the murder) let us sail right past, with a murmur about the chief of police being there already and expecting us.

Les Tilman was just getting out of his car as we arrived. I introduced him to Shirley; they were pleased to meet each other face to face.

"Well, here I am," he told me. "I don't know what I said, I was talking so fast, but Mr. Whitten bought it. Now you tell me why I'm being taken away from my wife and my TV set."

"You'll hear it when everybody else does."

Les shrugged, then worked the door knocker. A servant admitted us. Shirley sort of crouched down behind me—she didn't want to get noticed and evicted. She figured she belonged there by virtue of her great curiosity.

The butler or whatever he was addressed himself exclusively to Les. Apparently, my status here was no secret below stairs. He also ignored Spot completely, which was rather tough, considering the dog had been born there. We were led into the parlor. The chief nodded a greeting. Brenda said hi. She was sitting in a chair, looking sick, holding on to her crutches for dear life. Grant was at the sideboard pouring something amber into a couple of glasses. He handed one to the old man.

I watched that with a certain amount of interest. The chief was playing it cagey, apparently, saving Grant's face with Mr. Whitten, if only for the time being.

The chief kept giving me significant looks, as though he expected something from me, God knew what.

A. Lawrence Whitten took a long pull at his drink. "I would offer you some, but you are not a guest. Cooper has arranged this, and it's easier to get it over with than to fight. I hope you'll be brief."

Not brief enough to suit me. "Yes, sir," I said.

I tasted bile, swallowed to get rid of it. Then I cleared my throat. *Come on, Cobb,* I told myself savagely, *spit it out.*

That's pretty much what I did. "I'm going back to New York tomorrow," I said.

"Good riddance," Grant said.

I looked at him. Grant was playing it deadpan. I wondered how much he knew about my part in his impending downfall. Or did he still think he could charm his way out of the downfall altogether? I dismissed it. Grant had nothing to do with my business tonight. Or so I thought.

"From your point of view, I deserve that," I said. "And maybe from my point of view, too." In a very real way, I knew this mess was my fault. "If I had this past week to live over, I'd do it far away from my old alma mater."

"Get to the point, Cobb," Mr. Whitten said. I had a sudden flash of déjà vu to another meeting like this; another old man, another sad daughter.

But I shook that off, too. "Yes," I said, "the point. I have been running around this town, making a nuisance of myself, in an attempt to find new evidence to clear Dan Morris of murdering Debra Whitten. I thought I'd found some on Sunday afternoon, when an attempt was made on my life. But that turned out to be the result of another matter entirely."

"I'm not surprised," the old man muttered. I ignored him and took another peek at Grant. He was still playing it cool. To hell with him.

On with the show. I was getting to the hard part. I was supposed to be in control of things here, but the futility and the goddam stupid *waste* of it all was clogging my throat and making it hard to talk. I had to force the words past it. I'll bet it made my voice sound very compelling. I was getting sick of it.

"I have come to the conclusion that there was no new evidence—"

Behind me, I heard Shirley gasp. It was the first uncool, unprofessional thing she'd ever done.

"—that the story was all there to read that night. That I've just been too stubborn and blind to see it."

"Do you mean to say," Chief Cooper said, "that you now think your friend killed Miss Whitten?"

I turned to meet his eyes. "Yes," I said. "My friend killed Miss Whitten. It was a crime of passion, committed in anger on the spur of the moment. But the deception and lying since then have been deliberate. And let me tell you something. When someone who's supposed to be your friend lets you run around making a goddam fool of yourself, it does something to you."

"Excuse me," a voice cut it. It was Les Tilman, who until now had been effacing himself in a corner of the room. "I'm no lawyer or anything," the reporter went on, "but I know this town. If you go back to New York tomorrow, and leave Dan Morris in the lurch, you might as well be turning the key on him yourself."

"So?" I said. "Doesn't he deserve to have the key turned on him?"

Brenda Whitten spoke for the first time. Her voice was barely a whisper. "Matt," she said helplessly. "No—"

I turned on her. "Why not?" She shook her head, starting to cry. It occurred to me I'd spent a good part of the week making this kid cry. I knelt in front of her and cradled a limp hand in my freshly bandaged ones. Spot came over to lend moral support. "Come on, Junebug," I said softly. "Tell me, please. Why not?"

It went on that way for some seconds. Once, Mr. Whitten was about to command me to stop. I didn't dare look away from Brenda's face, but I found out later the chief had shut the old man up.

"Brenda, please. You're my friend, aren't you? Dan's friend?"

I heard Les Tilman say, "His friend. Holy Christ. *His friend.*"

"Brenda, tell me. You weren't going to let Dan go to prison, were you?"

She just shook her head some more, and said, *"I can't!"*

"All right, baby, all right. You didn't mean to kill her, I know that. But what happened?"

"She laughed at me!" She practically screamed it. "She was always laughing at me. She was so beautiful and healthy—and she made such a big deal of her lousy skin condition!"

Inside, I was shouting derision at myself. The body hadn't cooled off yet, and there was Spot, licking Debbie's face. *For a long time.* Yet earlier in the week he'd taken one lick and started to choke, put off by the medicated makeup. I'd forgotten all about it until Spot licked lighter fluid off Eve's face in the woods.

Probably because I'd *wanted* to forget it. Because I liked Brenda. But there was no getting around it. Dogs don't lie. Spot was licking that face because there was no makeup on it, period. But Debbie was very fastidious about her makeup. No one saw her without it, except for the immediate family and her lover.

Not Dan. He'd complained to me that very afternoon about it. So if Dan walked Debbie back to the house, and argued with her and killed her, *when had she taken off her makeup?* The police theory had to be wrong.

So who'd been in the house with Debbie? Dan, then Brenda, then me. And she was dead when I got there. Grant had been on the grounds, but nobody's evidence could put him in the house. And Brenda, who had no reason to protect him as far as I could see, definitely put him *out.*

Besides, Grant was excluded for another reason, a reason

that almost made me want to laugh. Grant *couldn't* have
delivered that flesh-crushing blow, that awesome display of
strength that killed Debbie. And it just so happened Brenda
could.

"Why did she laugh at you?" I asked the killer in my
gentlest voice.

"I—I was just trying to talk *sense* to her. To make her see
how foolish she was to want Grant when Dan loved her so
much. She treated Dan so badly. When I walked in the
house, I saw the broken banister—I knew she must have
done something awful to him. She told me to mind my own
business, but this *was* my business. *It was!*"

"We believe you, Junebug," I said.

That seemed to soothe her. She didn't look at her father
or at anyone but me. Her friend. Spot made a sympathetic
noise in his throat.

"It was my business because—because I knew something
about Grant."

Grant again. I risked breaking eye contact with Brenda to
get a look at him. He wasn't quite so cool.

But he was trying. "This child," he said, "is obviously in
a lot of distress."

"Just like *you* were!" Brenda yelled. It was an explosion
of pure loathing. "The night of the engagement party. When
you were drunk and I felt sorry for you and you told me how
pretty I was and how nice I was, nicer—nicer than Debbie.
And how the leg didn't matter to you."

The look of disgust left her face when she looked back at
me.

"I told Debbie all of this, Matt. I tried to make her see. I
told her how he took me in the back seat and made lo—no,
how he *stuck* it in me! There was no love in it. There's *never*
love in it. I've found that out since. Not for me, anyway. I
was crying, and he was making me swear not to tell anyone."

I did a little subtraction. Brenda had been fourteen years old at the time. I carefully avoided looking at Grant Sewall because if I had laid eyes on him, nothing would have been able to keep me from killing him.

"And when I told Debbie she laughed. She—she called me a liar. Then she said, Grant would never get *that* drunk, and she laughed at me some more, and I got so mad I just hit her, I just swung my crutch like a baseball bat and hit her and she fell, and I started to scream—"

Somebody else started to scream. Her father, a rasping cry of anger from a communicator who'd run out of words. He was going for Grant, and it would have been interesting to see what he did when he got there, but of course Chief Cooper wrapped him up before he could.

Brenda was sobbing. She reached out to me, to *me*, for Jesus's sweet sake, the way she had in Dan's apartment. I put my arms around her as she buried her face against my shoulder as if to hide from the world and everything in it.

I was looking at Grant. Everyone was looking at Grant. Chief Cooper had a look of disgust on his face, as if he'd suddenly found himself in a room with a million maggots.

He was the one who spoke first. "Christ, Sewall," he said. "You're no goddam good at all, are you?"

Grant said nothing. He just swallowed and fixed his tie and wiped some sweat from his handsome forehead.

Brenda held me tighter, and cried as if she would never stop.

CHAPTER 29

"Get back in the box!"
—Señor Wences, "The Ed Sullivan Show" (CBS)

A doctor came and gave Brenda a tranquilizer, and some cops came and hauled Grant in, ostensibly on charges associated with the ComCab thing, but really because the chief all of a sudden decided a bastard like that ought to be in jail.

I was making a break for it. I needed some air. Les Tilman was sneaking out, too. I spoke to him on the steps.

"There's your story, Les," I said.

"If Mr. Whitten lets you print it," Shirley added. She used to work for a congressman, so she has a tendency to think of things like that.

"It'll be printed," Les said grimly. "I'll get it out even if I have to buy a job shop and set the type myself. Nobody's going to be able to hush this up, don't worry. But Cobb, may I say something?"

"What?"

"I hope to hell I never piss you off. You are one scary son of a bitch."

That about did it. That was just the sort of thing I needed to hear to make my life complete. "Go to hell, Les," I told him.

"Can I quote you?"

"I'll give you something to quote. Let me out of here."

I got in the car and asked Shirley to drive to the county jail. Eve was going to meet us there and get me in to see Dan.

About halfway there, Shirley said, "Matt, there's something I've got to tell you."

I leaned back in my seat. "If you think I'm scary, save it."

"No, it wasn't that. Harris never put through your resignation."

"What?"

"He figured you were being hasty. When you called in and said you were quitting your job, he put you down for sick time. He would have told you when we first got here, but you hurt his feelings."

I had thought I would never laugh again, but all of a sudden there I was, roaring until tears came to my eyes. Not only had I wrecked a life or two this week, I'd even wind up getting paid for it.

Wonderful. Now I had something to live for.

Spot waited in the car with Shirley while I went in to talk to Dan. Eve was already there, talking to the chief. They were trying to get a judge on the phone to authorize Dan's release.

The chief showed me to Dan's cell. He looked like he'd just been sentenced, not cleared. He greeted me listlessly and told me to sit down.

It made me mad. "You're welcome!" I snapped.

"Oh, Matt, of course. You're the best friend I could imagine, let alone have. But Chief Cooper was just in here. He says it was Brenda who killed Debbie. Then he rushed away."

"He's trying to get you out of here."

There was a puzzled look in Dan's big sad eyes. "But how could it be *Brenda*? I just don't see it."

I showed it to him. He didn't like it any better than I did.

"All right, it had to be her because of that makeup, but the blow, Matt. How could she do *that*?"

"You taught her how. I saw you doing it the first day I was here."

"What? I never taught her *shuto*."

"No, but you taught her *baseball*. That nice, compact, powerful left-handed swing. She used her crutch, her stainless steel crutch. It's lighter than a baseball bat but longer. High school physics—longer moment arm, more force. Much more force than you can generate with just your body, if you aren't a black belt."

Dan was scratching his beard and saying of course.

"Yeah," I said, "of course. Plenty of room to swing in that wide hallway, and one moment of anger and bam. And the wise old Medical Examiner immediately said it was a karate blow. What else could it have been? What else has a rounded striking surface with a solid core covered with padding? What else, but a human hand? Well, how about a tube of stainless steel, curved and padded to fit comfortably under your arm?"

Dan shook his head. "The poor kid," he said.

"Yes. But we spent all that time thinking, or trying to think, of some sort of weapon someone might have used. And there was Brenda, right there, with *two* of them. Perfectly disguised. I was so used to seeing her with them— hell, in a very real way, they were *part* of her. It was all there for me to see the first second after I arrived. Spot licking Debbie's un-madeup face, and Brenda standing there on her crutches, shocked and crying."

"The poor kid," he said again.

"Yes, Dan." For no reason, I was getting irritated with

him. "But she killed her sister, no matter how. It had to come out, and you know it."

"But she must have been through *hell* this past week!"

"And what have *you* been through? Disneyland?"

"That's not fair, Matt."

"Murder isn't fair."

"Did you have to put her through the wringer like that? In front of *everybody?* Couldn't you just—"

"Couldn't I just *what?* Frame Grant? I might have at that if I could have gotten away with it. But let's be real. Clear you without involving her? Not bloody likely. Do you think I enjoyed doing this? Maybe I should have just forgotten all about it and let you take the rap for her. That's what *she* was going to do.

"The really amusing part of it is that she never thought of getting away with it, Dan, or framing you. She didn't think of anything at all. She was just *standing* there, shocked at what she'd done when I rushed in, saw that bruise on Debbie's throat, and decided you'd killed her. Brenda was ready to tell me then, but I was busy being worried about getting you a lawyer, so she shut up and let Nature take its course. So, in a way," I concluded, "I'm responsible for your being here in the first place!"

"Then you *did* think I killed her!"

"Yes, goddammit, I did!" I exploded. "I'm sorry, Dan, but there it is. I saw what it looked like, and I was scared to death for you. It lasted until I spoke to you on the phone, but until then, yes, I thought you did it."

Dan looked grim. "Don't worry about it. When I heard some of the evidence, I began to think I might have done it myself. But dammit, Matt, you've practically *crucified* Brenda! The kid lost her head for one second, and look what she's in for now."

"And in that second, she killed the woman you loved." I waved that aside before Dan could get mad. "All right, forget about that. But look at the situation I was in back there in the woods, when Spot and Fred Stampe so kindly led me to the truth. Stampe had said, 'Weapons are everywhere,' and it clicked.

"Brenda had killed her sister, but *I* was the one who gave her the idea, in her moment of panic, to blame it on you. She would have come apart and confessed and faced the music, which at that time probably wouldn't have been so bad.

"And Dan, if she hadn't been so scared, she wouldn't have let you stay in jail. Subconsciously, she was confessing all damn week. She called my attention to her crutches, constantly. At one point, when she was trying to pretend you had done it, she said, 'Dan, *should* have killed her.' Not 'He was *right* to have killed her,' but 'He *should* have.'

"Brenda's a careful speaker; she doesn't make that kind of diction mistake. Unconsciously, she was saying exactly what she meant. You *should* have killed her; then *she* wouldn't have had to. You would be in prison justly, and she could feel sorry for you, and everything would be the way it was supposed to be.

"And she'd still be rid of Debbie. Who had two legs. Who had your love. Who had given her Grant, then taken him back. You should have killed her, Dan, because deep down, Brenda wanted her dead. What she didn't want was the guilt.

"And yet, she *wanted* me to figure it out. She showed me she had some kind of hold over Grant. He sure as hell didn't want to talk to me at the cemetery Saturday afternoon, but Brenda made him do it by getting stern with him. I wondered about it at the time, but I didn't follow up. He was afraid of her about something. Now we know.

"Hell, Brenda even called my attention to Debbie's skin condition!"

I sat down on the edge of Dan's cot. "You know something? I bet that if this had been a Network case, with a bunch of strangers involved, I would have gotten it before Spot had taken his last lick at Debbie's face. I just didn't want to think of Brenda as the killer. I wouldn't *let* myself do it, not seriously. I remember how happy I was when I thought I'd cleared her by proving she couldn't have delivered that karate blow."

I laughed at myself. Dan said, "But you learned the truth eventually. Why couldn't you just tell the police or something?"

I nodded. "I could have. But I figured that because I was at least partially responsible for the mess she was in, I owed it to her to do it the way I did. Eve tried to talk me out of it."

"*Owed* it to her? Matt, are you nuts? You've probably *destroyed* her."

"Maybe," I said. "But if I'd gone to Cooper with it, what would have happened? He might not have believed it—it's not like I had any evidence or anything—and even if he had, he would have come at Brenda like an adversary. She would have been scared. She would have kept lying. You'd be convicted in the meantime, most likely, and by then, no one would believe you hadn't done it no matter who confessed to anything.

"Besides, despite everything, she's not a bad kid. I'd given her the idea of letting you take the rap; I had to try to make her see how lousy that idea was, how mean. I pretended to turn on you, made some pointed remarks about what a friend is supposed to do.

"It got to her. I had to help her a little, but she came through. I owed her a chance to do that."

Dan came at me, his mouth like an open wound in the middle of his beard. "*You goddam hypocrite!*" he spat. "You sanctimonious bastard! You mean you can actually stand there and tell me you raked that kid over the coals to save her *soul?*"

"I did it, goddammit, to give her a chance, in a future that looks almighty bleak, to be able to live with herself! And incidentally," I added, "to save your ungrateful ass!"

The chief came in. "Hey, let the other prisoners sleep, will you?" He shrugged, then said, "Mr. Morris, I'm sorry, there's no way you can be released before morning. All the judges have their phones off the hook or something."

Dan, still seething, said he didn't really mind. "I'll look around the place and memorize it. In the future, I can remind myself of where I almost spent the rest of my life."

I got up. "Dan," I began.

He smiled at me through his beard. "I know, I know, partner. I'm grateful, I really am. I need some time to let it sink in, that's all." The smile fell from his face. "Is anything going to happen to Grant?"

"It will if I can help it," the chief said. "I'll tell you one thing. He's through with Whitten Communications. And I'll nail that bastard on this corruption thing if it kills me. Any help Cobb wants to give me on the New York end of things will be appreciated."

"You've got it," I told him. I said good-bye to Dan. He saw I couldn't shake hands, so he got up and gave me a hug. I started to mist up, and I really didn't give a damn if Cooper saw tears in my eyes or not.

I was about through the door when Dan said, "Matt?"

"What is it, partner?"

"Life stinks sometimes, doesn't it?"

"Yeah," I conceded. "But consider the alternative."

CHAPTER 30

"Good-bye for now, and may Gawd bless."
—Red Skelton, "The Red Skelton Hour" (CBS)

Eve was angry she couldn't get Dan out tonight, but happy her client had been vindicated. She kissed me quickly, then went in to speak to him about his release tomorrow.

When she came back down, I said, "Rendering your bill, huh?"

"I always wait a week before I do that. I've got to make a phone call when we get home—back to Dan's place, I mean."

"To the judge?"

"No, that's hopeless. I'm supposed to call Mr. Whitten for Dan and tell him no hard feelings, and if there's anything he can do for Brenda, all he has to do is ask."

That was my second big laugh of the night. That schmuck, that softhearted, softheaded, impossible schmuck. God bless him, I thought.

Because if anyone owed Brenda anything, *I* was the one. All the time Cobb, the Grand Inquisitor, was pulling the admission from her, Brenda never threw my own guilt at me, never made me acknowledge that I had been the one to give her the idea that my best friend could have been the murderer. I thought about it all during the time we spent getting Spot from Shirley and arranging for me to ride with her back to New York tomorrow.

"You're going home," Eve said.

"Yes, but I'll be back."

"Of course," she said. "You'll be the star witness at Brenda Whitten's trial." By this time, she knew all the details of what had gone on.

"If Brenda Whitten ever stands trial for anything, I will eat a gavel. With mayonnaise. Between her father's juice, her pretty self, and that genuinely horrible story she has to tell, she'll be able to cop to a manslaughter beef and get a suspended sentence. If she doesn't walk for temporary insanity. You're the lawyer around here, what do you think?"

"I think you're right," Eve said. "I don't know how I feel about that." I knew how I felt about it. Even if jail was no part of her future, I wouldn't want to trade places with Brenda Whitten for all her father's millions.

I smiled at Eve. "You're not supposed to feel about it. You're a lawyer. But trial or no trial, I'm coming back anyway. Resolved: Relationships with smart, tough, brave, freckled women who care for a man should be pursued, even if they do have careers that will keep them four hundred miles away from said man most of the time. You take the negative."

"Not on your life," she said. She pulled the car over, set the emergency brake, took me in her arms, and kissed me.

It was wonderful, and it came just when I needed it. I tried to lose myself in Eve's embrace, and forget about a little girl who'd clung to me that night, looking for comfort I couldn't give her.

For a second I almost did forget, but I never would. Not completely. To save a friend, I'd set off Truth like a bomb, and the shrapnel had wounded everybody in sight, in one way or another. Even Dan. Even me. I wondered where Justice fit into all of this.

But I could drive myself crazy that way.

So I'd spend one more night with this wonderful woman at my side. Tomorrow, I'd meet my friend outside the jail and see him a free man before I had to go. I'd take him to the House of Hans for a lunch we could pay for. Then I'd kiss Eve good-bye, shake Dan's hand if I could manage it. If they'd let me, I'd say good-bye to a poor little girl who'd gotten angry at her sister, and tell her—God knows what. I'd tell her something. Then I'd get into the car with Spot and Shirley, and ride back to New York. Back to the Network. Back to the problems of people I didn't care much about—they were always easier to deal with. Back to the familiar places, the familiar people.

Back, in short, to what passes in my life for normal.

But with a difference. Now there was a little portion of my mind that would stay in Sewanka. In the custody of a red-haired lady lawyer. With freckles.

MORE MYSTERIOUS PLEASURES

HAROLD ADAMS
MURDER
Carl Wilcox debuts in a story of triple murder which exposes the underbelly of corruption in the town of Corden, shattering the respectability of its most dignified citizens. #501 $3.50

THE NAKED LIAR
When a sexy young widow is framed for the murder of her husband, Carl Wilcox comes through to help her fight off cops and big-city goons. #420 $3.95

THE FOURTH WIDOW
Ex-con/private eye Carl Wilcox is back, investigating the death of a "popular" widow in the Depression-era town of Corden, S.D. #502 $3.50

EARL DERR BIGGERS
THE HOUSE WITHOUT A KEY
Charlie Chan debuts in the Honolulu investigation of an expatriate Bostonian's murder. #421 $3.95

THE CHINESE PARROT
Charlie Chan works to find the key to murders seemingly without victims—but which have left a multitude of clues. #503 $3.95

BEHIND THAT CURTAIN
Two murders sixteen years apart, one in London, one in San Francisco, each share a major clue in a pair of velvet Chinese slippers. Chan seeks the connection. #504 $3.95

THE BLACK CAMEL
When movie goddess Sheila Fane is murdered in her Hawaiian pavilion, Chan discovers an interrelated crime in a murky Hollywood mystery from the past. #505 $3.95

CHARLIE CHAN CARRIES ON
An elusive transcontinental killer dogs the heels of the Lofton Round the World Cruise. When the touring party reaches Honolulu, the murderer finally meets his match. #506 $3.95

JULIE SMITH
TRUE-LIFE ADVENTURE
Paul McDonald earned a meager living ghosting reports for a San Francisco private eye until the gumshoe turned up dead . . . now the killers are after him.   #407 $3.95

TOURIST TRAP
A lunatic is out to destroy San Francisco's tourism industry; can feisty lawyer/sleuth Rebecca Schwartz stop him while clearing an innocent man of a murder charge?   #533 $3.95

ROSS H. SPENCER
THE MISSING BISHOP
Chicago P.I. Buzz Deckard has a missing person to find. Unfortunately his client has disappeared as well, and no one else seems to be who or what they claim.   #416 $3.50

MONASTERY NIGHTMARE
Chicago P.I. Luke Lassiter tries his hand at writing novels, and encounters murder in an abandoned monastery.   #534 $3.50

REX STOUT
UNDER THE ANDES
A long-lost 1914 fantasy novel from the creator of the immortal Nero Wolfe series. "The most exciting yarn we have read since *Tarzan of the Apes.*"—*All-Story Magazine*.   #419 $3.50

ROSS THOMAS
CAST A YELLOW SHADOW
McCorkle's wife is kidnapped by agents of the South African government. The ransom—his cohort Padillo must assassinate their prime minister.   #535 $3.95

THE SINGAPORE WINK
Ex-Hollywood stunt man Ed Cauthorne is offered $25,000 to search for colleague Angelo Sacchetti—a man he thought he'd killed in Singapore two years earlier.   #536 $3.95

THE FOOLS IN TOWN ARE ON OUR SIDE
Lucifer Dye, just resigned from a top secret U.S. Intelligence post, accepts a princely fee to undertake the corruption of an entire American city.   #537 $3.95

JIM THOMPSON
THE KILL-OFF
Luanne Devore was loathed by everyone in her small New England town. Her plots and designs threatened to destroy them—unless they destroyed her first.   #538 $3.95

DAVID WILLIAMS' "MARK TREASURE" SERIES

UNHOLY WRIT

London financier Mark Treasure helps a friend reaquire some property. He stays to unravel the mystery when a Shakespeare manuscript is discovered and foul murder done.   #112 $3.95

TREASURE BY DEGREES

Mark Treasure discovers there's nothing funny about a board game called "Funny Farms." When he becomes involved in the takeover struggle for a small university, he also finds there's nothing funny about murder.   #113 $3.95

■ ■